S0-AJL-623

j H1802 ti

3 0250 00384 5992

Titania's
Lodestone

TITANIA'S LODESTONE

Gail Hamilton

Atheneum ❦ 1975 ❦ New York

Copyright © 1975 by Gail Hamilton
All rights reserved
Published simultaneously in Canada by
McClelland & Stewart, Ltd.
Manufactured in the United States of America
Printed by Sentry Press, New York
Bound by The Book Press, Inc.
Brattleboro, Vermont
Designed by Harriett Barton
First Edition

LIBRARY OF CONGRESS CATALOGING IN PUBLICATION DATA

Hamilton, Gail. Titania's lodestone.

SUMMARY: Priscilla's vagabond family finds an unexpected
home in Massachusetts but not until Priscilla accepts herself
and her unusual family does she find contentment.
[1. Family life—Fiction]   I. Title.
PZ7.H18156Ti   [Fic]   74-19491
ISBN 0-689-30449-8

for

JEAN KARL

Titania's
Lodestone

ONE

PRISCILLA pushed her sleeping brother over to his side of the van and reached for the case containing her journals. Up in front her mother, Hazel, was asleep. All Priscilla could see of her was the baggy visored cap she had bought in Finland. It had looked all right there because so many women wore them, but in America it looked odd. Still, Priscilla was used to Hazel's looking odd. Her father, Paul, was hunched over the steering wheel, his dark ponytail hanging down the middle of his back. He had been driving all afternoon in the pouring rain.

She found the flashlight and turned it on, aiming it down so Paul wouldn't complain about not being able to see. The only time he ever got cross, almost, was when he drove. Once he and Hazel had had a fight right on the banks of the Rhine near Coblenz because he had been so crabby. Afterward he bought her a big armful of flowers, and she got him a book by Kirkegaard. Most of the time Paul was a tolerant and understanding person.

Priscilla pushed aside her brother Peter's knapsack, wondering what he had in it that made it so heavy. Probably rocks. He saved interesting rocks. She reached under a pile of parkas and raincoats, but the case of journals wasn't there. She got on her knees and rummaged. The wheels of the Fiat van made a swishing sound on the wet turnpike. Rain drummed on the roof, and the windshield wipers scraped and squeaked on the streaming glass.

Priscilla began to feel a little panicky. What if the journals had been lost? She knew she had had them when she came through customs. She always carried them herself, just as Hazel carried the little box with the lodestone in it. (Once the customs man had said, "What's in there?" and Hazel had said, "Oh, that's just my casket." He had looked very startled.) Priscilla moved Paul's camera case and felt behind it. Relief! She could feel the smooth leather case that held her journals.

She worked the case free and sat down with her back to the driver's seat. She pulled out the first book, and the other three fell into her lap. She opened Volume One and looked at her neat handwriting. "The Early Years" was the title, with a subtitle that said, "Recorded After the Fact, as Remembered by the Author of these Journals, Looking Back From the Age of Thirteen." She had written this one almost two years ago, during the first of the long winters in Finland. The table of contents read:

> 1 I Am Born. Under Unusual Circumstances to Say the Least

They were the kind of blank books people used to keep accounts in, but Priscilla had carefully crossed out "Paid" and "Received." Each of the other books dealt with one of the last three years. The current one was called "Finland—Phase Two," and now she turned to a blank page and wrote, "Homeward the Travelers Wend Their Weary Way: Maine Revisited." She looked down at the clean page, trying to imagine what the book would hold by the end of the year. The rest of the family dreaded the return to Maine, but for her it was coming home to paradise.

"It is nearly 6:00 P.M.," she wrote, propping the flashlight between her knees, "on the thirteenth day of August. It is raining. Leaves will soon be turning. A year ago we were in Lapland, and the leaves had just begun to turn . . ." And it was so beautiful, she thought, so beautiful. She thought of the family from Helsinki, whose parents had lived in Karelia until the Russian occupation drove them out. The girl—what was her name?—had taught Priscilla and Peter some Russian words in exchange for American. Priscilla had liked Finland the best of all the places they had lived. She knew she would miss it. But she was an American and she wanted more than anything to establish her roots, though Paul smiled and said that made her sound like a turnip. Turning to her journal again she wrote: "Tomorrow we will be in Surrey." If the oil didn't spring another leak. The Fiat was fairly new but it was secondhand and it had problems.

Surrey before morning. It was hard to believe. Back to the old house her grandfather had left them, the house across the road from the sea, where her father had been born and Parkinses had lived for generations. When she was ten, they had spent most of one year there. She hardly remembered the things the others remembered: how ramshackle the house had become, how cold it got, how isolated they were. They were only going back now because they had inherited the house and Paul thought they could either rebuild the house or tear it down and put up a cottage for summer renters. But Priscilla thought that once they were there, she might be able to persuade them to stay. They would feel then the things she remembered: the pleasure of being on home ground, the smell of the sea, the singing of the wind, the kind of people who accepted them because they were Parkinses. They didn't care that Paul wore his hair long or that Hazel wore odd clothes and went in for meditation. Such things were no stranger to them than Harry Wetherbee's fondness for strong drink or Allan Bates's smallpox scars. They belonged. Priscilla was the Parkins girl and Peter was the Parkins boy, "who looks a sight like his granddad." They accepted Paul's reason for the years in Europe—that he and his wife felt more comfortable there because there wasn't so much fuss about money and material things. They only drew the line at calling Hazel "Titania," and that was not because they thought it was silly but because they found it troublesome to pronounce.

They accepted Hazel's explanation, or Paul's for her, that when she married him, she discovered that the name Hazel Parkins added up numerologically to a portent of death by suffocation. It was an unpleasant idea, so after working with the numbers and signs for a long time, Hazel had changed her name to Titania. A few years ago Priscilla had started calling her Hazel, to show she didn't believe in numerology and to satisfy a little unexpressed superstition of her own that it was unlucky not to call things by their right names. Hazel didn't seem to mind, nor did she object when Peter called her "Mom," although she said "Mom" was shorthand for Male Chauvinism and Enslavement of Women. Priscilla never knew when Hazel meant things like that and when she was joking.

She put the journals back in the leather case, cleared a place on the steamy window and tried to see out. Paul, who hated all freeways, interchanges, carriageways, turnpikes, and autobahns, had turned off the Newburyport Turnpike and was following a winding road through the country. They were still in Massachusetts and then there would be that little edge of New Hampshire to cross before they were in Maine. Then Kennebunk, Biddeford, Saco . . ."

"Where are we?" Peter yawned and sat up. "Turku? Heidelberg? Copenhagen? Hey, my foot's gone to sleep."

They passed a cluster of stores. "The sign says RYAL SIDE," Priscilla said. "We're in Ryal Side."

"What's a side? What country are we in?"

Priscilla kicked him. "Where do you think? We're on Jupiter."

"Well, why didn't somebody tell me? Quit kicking people."

"You said your foot was asleep. I was being helpful."

His answer was lost in a loud clunking sound in the Fiat's engine.

"Gad, what was that?"

Paul slowed way down and drove with his head cocked toward the window, listening. Hazel was still asleep.

"Paul will fix it," Priscilla said. They had grown up believing that their father, who was an expert mechanic and a skillful carpenter, could fix anything. He could also explain anything to them, from the structure of the atom to the best way to play a hand of poker.

The Fiat made a left turn and passed an old, wooden factory. Across the road there was a square nineteenth-century building, a clubhouse of some kind, with a golf course and tennis courts. Rain stood in puddles on the courts. Priscilla stopped looking out, but Peter kept his nose against the cold glass as they swung back onto Route 1A.

"Gas stations," he reported. "Liquor store. Bars. Restaurants. Hamburger stands. More gas stations."

She looked over his shoulder. "How about that?" She pointed to a seventeenth-century house, its dark clapboards gleaming in the rain. "That's a nice house." She always defended America, and Peter always defended Europe.

"Neon," he said, pointing ahead of them at a cluster of stores.

The neon bothered her too. You saw some in Europe, but not much. Advertising signs were mostly small and informative, not garish. But America was a lot more than neon and hamburger stands.

"We just passed a big lake," Peter said. It was getting almost too dark to see. "It had woods all around. Pretty."

"If you like woods and lakes, why are you so set against Maine?"

"I like to look at them, not live in them." Peter was a true child of Paul and Hazel. He would rather have a balcony seat at the opera than inherit an ancestral home. He'd rather try to communicate with a German or a Frenchman, a Russian, even a Finn, than listen to old-timers' stories about his forebears. He'd as soon live in a van or a tent and eat rice and yogurt as have one of Grandfather's lobster dinners. Well, all Priscilla wanted, she thought, was one thing, and it didn't seem too much to ask. She wanted to stay put and be like other people. When she'd said that to her parents not long ago, Hazel had said to Paul, "Where have we failed?"

There was a clank, louder than the first one, and the van lurched to a stop. Priscilla was thrown against the box that held Titania's lodestone. She put out her hand to steady it.

"How jolly," Peter said. "We've broken down in front of a garage."

TWO

PAUL sat hunched over the wheel, and Priscilla knew he was quietly cussing. Hazel sat up and scrubbed the sleep from her eyes. Paul opened the door on his side.

Priscilla watched him anxiously. He'll look under the bonnet, she thought, and fix it, and we'll get to Maine all right. No, "hood," not "bonnet." In the States a bonnet is a hood, and a boot is a trunk. She was trying to remember things like that so her speech would sound like other people's, not foreign. She had heard that Americans didn't think too much of foreignness. And an American who had lived most of her life abroad was, as her grandfather would have said, "neither fish, fowl, nor good red herring."

Paul took the flashlight from her and got out, Peter with him. It made Priscilla nervous to see them standing there as if they were at a funeral. Here lies the Fiat . . . She crawled out past the luggage, as Peter had done.

The rain gave her a wet slap across the face. She

closed the tailgate and stood against the van, slightly protected from the weather. They were on a block of stores and businesses, on a street that ran at right angles to the main road. Across the street was a magazine and newspaper store with a lunch counter. The sign said PAPER STORE. Somebody was having coffee at the counter inside. Another man, coat collar turned up, ran in and bought a paper and ran out again to the shelter of his car.

Next to the paper store stood a three-story building that had HENDERSON BLOCK—1913 cut into the granite slab over the entrance. The shop on the ground floor was a tailor's, with a big picture in the window of a woman in a riding habit. Up the street the lights went out in a hardware store, and then in a minute the small grocery store went dark. It was a town that proved Peter wrong. She couldn't see a hamburger stand, gas station, or even a motel. If the Fiat couldn't run, where would they sleep? Often they slept in the van, but they couldn't do that unless they could get it out of the downtown.

She moved around the van to see what Paul was doing. He straightened up and started toward the garage. A worklight still burned inside, but the big doors were closed. Paul knocked on the small entrance door. Nothing happened. Peter joined him and pounded on the door. Hazel put her head out of the window till the rain beating in her face made her pull it in again.

The door opened a crack and a man peered out at them, narrowing his eyes against the dark. "Closed," he said. As he began to pull the door shut, Paul caught it.

Priscilla couldn't hear what Paul said, but she saw the man look past him at the van. "Got no Fiat parts. I'd have to send for 'em." He started to shut the door.

Priscilla moved nearer to hear what Paul was saying.

The man took off the black mechanic's cap he was wearing and scratched his thin, sandy hair. "Could take six months if they have to send to the factory."

Paul looked into the garage. "You're working on a Rover."

"Yeah, blasted thing. That's what I mean. I want no more to do with foreign cars than I can help. But that belongs to Mrs. Wentworth, so I got to fix it, somehow." In his sudden flow of complaint, he stepped back. Paul at once moved in, Peter behind him and Priscilla tentatively behind Peter, ready to flee if the man objected to their coming in. The garage had two American cars in it, partly dismantled, and under the worklight in the center of the floor stood a late-model Rover with the bonnet up.

Paul went to it casually and looked in. He reached into the engine and jiggled something.

"Here, don't monkey with that car," the man said. "I got troubles enough." He stepped toward Paul, his grease-blackened fists on his hips. He was a short, fat man. Nailed to a beam over his head was a sign that said PUDDLEFORD FORD AGENCY. *Buy Your Ford from Pud.*

Ignoring the man, Paul said to Peter, "See? That's the trouble."

The man got angry. "Look, mister, the garage is closed. I told you. Now git."

"The trouble here—" Paul began in a reasonable voice.

"I'll worry about the trouble here." He jerked his thumb toward the door. "Out."

"I can fix the Rover," Paul said.

The man's face was getting red. "You take your kids and beat it before I call the cop. Now I mean it."

Paul bent over the engine as if he had not heard the man. "Try it now, Peter."

Peter jumped into the driver's seat and turned the key. The engine caught and stalled.

The man roared at Paul. "By God, I'll have you thrown in the jug." He grabbed Paul's ponytail and pulled.

"Ow." Paul shook his head as if the man were a bothersome insect. "Don't do that." He called to Peter, "Gun it."

Priscilla could see Peter eagerly turning the key, but nothing happened. There was only a second or two of silence, but it was long enough for her to picture all of them huddled in a dank jail cell full of rats and criminals.

Then the Rover roared, sputtered, almost died, and settled into a steady purr. The man looked amazed. He stood still, forgetting to let go of Paul's hair.

Paul reached around and disengaged his hand. "If you don't mind." He had the happy little grin he always had when he made something work.

Peter sat at the wheel pretending he was driving the splendid Rover.

"Well, I'll be a son-of-a-gun." The man was no longer angry. "Was that luck or what?"

"Witchcraft," Peter said.

"I used to work on Rovers and Bentleys," Paul said, "one winter in Coventry."

One winter in Coventry. It had been a damp and dismal winter, but maybe now it would come in handy.

The man was studying Paul. "You know a lot about foreign cars, do you?"

"He only knows all there is to know," Peter said.

"I haven't worked too much on Japanese cars," Paul said. He was looking around the garage, looking at tools, hoists and supplies, as if the conversation didn't really interest him. But Priscilla hung on every word. If Paul could do a little work for this man while they were waiting for whatever the Fiat needed, then they could get to Maine all right, only a little late. Of course it wouldn't take any six months for the parts; garage men always said things like that.

The man circled around Paul as if he were thinking of buying him. Paul said, "Excuse me," and pushed past him to look at one of the American cars.

"You lived in Europe or something?" the man said.

"Oh, yes," Paul said carelessly.

"Where 'bouts?"

"Scandinavia, Germany, England, Austria . . ." Paul shrugged. "All over. We were there quite a few years."

"Can you work on Saabs?"

"Of course."

The man rubbed his chin, leaving another smear of

black grease. "Got quite a few Saabs. Volvo? You know Volvo?"

"He worked in the factory," Peter said.

The man got a crafty look. "I need a man. My foreign man quit on me."

"Is that right?" Paul didn't even look at him.

" 'Course I can't pay much, size of town this is . . ."

If the man could see, Priscilla thought, holding her breath, if he had X-ray eyes and could see inside Paul's wallet, he'd know he could have all four of us working, just for coffee and yogurt money. But Paul started for the door. And Priscilla knew his indifference was real. Money, he always said, would turn up. And whenever they really needed it, it did. Paul said it was Titania's lodestone that did it, and when she was little, Priscilla had believed implicitly in the power of the lodestone. Now of course she knew better. Money turned up because Paul was an expert who could always get a job.

"You want a job?" the man said.

Paul sighed and hesitated. "Well, I don't know. We were heading for Maine."

"You ain't going to get to Maine in a bus that won't run."

Paul gave him a sudden smile. He smiled rarely, but when he did, it was such a radiant smile, it always gave Priscilla a little jolt of surprise and pleasure, as if she had never seen it before.

"We usually," Paul said, "get to where we want to go, one way or another."

"By hook or by crook?"

Paul shook his head, still smiling. "By hook, you might say, but not by crook."

The man gave a snort of laughter. "Listen, I know you hippies. You're like Gypsies, work a little, steal a little; it's your life-style. And as long as you don't get caught, why not? Huh? Why not?"

Priscilla knew what he was up to; he was trying to find out if Paul would steal him blind. It made her so mad she could hardly stand still. Paul was the most honest man in the whole world.

Paul turned away, looking bored. "I'll get my van towed away in the morning. Is there a motel around here?"

"Hold on. You want a job? I'm offering you a job."

Paul had his hand on the doorknob. He didn't turn around. "I don't know. It would have to be temporary. As soon as the Fiat is ready to roll . . ."

The man laughed again. "I ain't too worried about that."

Paul looked at him. "What is your name?"

"My name?" He looked surprised.

"Yes. I would need to know your name."

"Puddleford. Joshua Puddleford. They call me Pud. And for that matter, who are you?"

"Paul Parkins." They shook hands.

"All right, Mr. Parsnip, you better tell your girl friend to come in out of the rain, and we'll push that heap onto the lot."

Paul's face tightened. "Get yourself another boy," he said. He pushed Peter and Priscilla toward the door.

"Hold on, hold on," the man said. "What ails you?"

"I don't appreciate slighting remarks about my wife, and my name is Parkins."

Priscilla shivered. She didn't want Paul to throw away the job, but she was thrilled when he acted like this. In her mind she heard the faint clatter of swords and the bark of dueling pistols.

Mr. Puddleford bounced up and down in a state of agitation. "Son, ain't you got any sense of humor? I was just kidding you. I thought all the young people nowadays . . . Hell's bells, man, I'll start you out at what the last man finished up at . . ."

Priscilla's moment of elation left her. Paul was going to turn down the job, and she knew they would be out there in the cold rain pushing the van down the road to some place where they could park it for the night. It might be miles. For a girl only fifteen years old, she thought, she had pushed far too many cars.

Paul shook his head and reached for the doorlatch, but before he could get it, the door opened and in a gust of rain and fresh air, Hazel stood in the doorway.

Mr. Puddleford gasped and took a step backward.

Hazel was five feet ten, about five inches taller than Mr. Puddleford, and she was wearing her wooden clogs with the high platform heels. Her baggy white cap sat squarely on the middle of her head, her dark hair falling in waves to her shoulders. She had on the short, brightly embroidered skirt from Lapland and the knee-length white cotton socks that the Finnish girls wear. Around her shoulders she held the black, scarlet, and silver shawl that she had knitted. Tucked under one arm was the casket that held the lodestone.

"Criminently!" said Mr. Puddleford.

Paul looked hard at Mr. Puddleford. "This is my wife," he said, very distinctly. "This is Titania."

"Heavens above," said Mr. Puddleford. He took off his greasy cap and bowed.

Hazel inclined her head like a gracious queen. "How do you do."

Mr. Puddleford began to regain his composure. "I do fine, madam, very fine. I was just offering your husband here a job in my garage."

"That was kind." Hazel looked at Paul. "We will probably need to stay here for a short time, until the Fiat gets on its feet."

" 'Gets on its feet,' " Mr. Puddleford chuckled. "That's a good one. Now Mr. Pars . . . Mr. Parkins, if you will just give me a hand, we'll push your van onto the lot. There's no motel for twelve miles, but I got a camper out here that I took in trade—didn't want the thing, but you know how it is, to make a sale. So you can use that, and park it in my east pasture."

"Pasture with cows in it?" Peter said. He was afraid of cows.

"No, son, no cows lately. The land just sets there. It's part of the king's grant given to the Westons; my great-great-you-name-it-granddaddy bought it from the Westons in 1782. I got the deed."

"You're an old family?" Hazel asked.

"Ma'am, there's been a Joshua Puddleford in this town since 1694." He was thrusting his arms into a raincoat. "All right, gentlemen, let's give the van a push and a shove."

Paul looked at Hazel. Ever so lightly she brushed the casket with her fingertips. Paul sighed and followed Mr. Puddleford out into the rain. Peter went with them.

Priscilla looked at her mother. Hazel never consciously played up to her audience; it was just that occasions and people drew from her the kind of response a good actress would make. She relaxed and pushed the cap back a little. "Well, that was providential, wasn't it?"

But Priscilla knew that she didn't mean "providential"; she really meant, "The lodestone has done it again."

"Not too," Priscilla said. "I want to go to Maine."

"But we do need, dear, wheels to get there."

"But tomorrow . . ." Priscilla began, wanting to say "Surely we can't live in a cow pasture, even without cows."

"Tomorrow," Hazel said, "we will consult the stars."

THREE

PRISCILLA awoke to sunshine streaming in the tiny windows of Mr. Puddleford's camper. For a moment she couldn't remember where she was, but that was a sensation she had long ago grown used to. She sat up on the tiny bunk and smelled a campfire. Oh yes. The king's grant.

She washed and dressed and climbed out. Her father was drinking a cup of coffee, and Peter was feeding folded newspapers into the Safari grill. Hazel was mixing pancake batter. A mist rose from the meadow, half obscuring the two-man tent where Peter and Paul had slept.

Priscilla wandered down a slope to a line of willows that bordered a river, a slow-moving, dark stream full of shadows. She thought about the people to whom the king had granted this land. What had happened to them? She hoped she'd get a chance to tell Mr. Puddleford that her family had lived in Surrey since 1772. She heard Hazel call her for breakfast, but Hazel always called a good ten minutes before things were ready. So Priscilla went on along the river a little farther. The tall grass was wet, and Priscilla's jeans were soon soaked to the knees. She sat down on a stump. Her worry now was that the Fiat wouldn't get fixed in time to reach Surrey before the first day of school. It was hard enough going to a strange school without arriving late, after everybody else knew where their homerooms were and what their locker combinations were, and all that. But in Maine the kids would be nice, and the teachers would be helpful. They would say to each other, "She's the Parkins young'un. The Parkinses have come back."

"Priscilla! Come eat." Hazel was calling again.

She got up from her dream of Maine and went back to the camper. Peter had piled some of their things inside the tent. Paul was eating breakfast and drinking his strong coffee. By the time Priscilla began to eat, he was leaving for the garage. She hoped he'd remember to get it settled about his salary. Who knew whether they could trust this Mr. Puddleford or not, and Paul was so indifferent to money.

After breakfast she noted in her journal what had happened so far, and then she joined Peter on an exploration. To the southwest, over a rise in the land they could see what must be the Puddleford house. It was a big old farmhouse with a central chimney. One shutter hung askew, and the house needed painting. The yard had several junked cars lying around. Near the barn some chickens scratched, and Priscilla saw a girl in cut-offs come out to feed them. It was hard to think of the place as a king's grant. She wondered if Mr. Puddleford had made that up.

When they were fairly close to the farmhouse, they turned around and walked upriver, Peter in front of Priscilla, striding along in his long-legged, loose way. Priscilla had to hurry to keep up with him.

"I can't see anything," she said, "if you charge along like a bull moose."

He waited for her to catch up. "Well, Shorty, when are you going to grow out of the dwarf stage?"

Everybody said, "She doesn't take after her parents, does she?" She hoped she never would, in that respect. She didn't want to be tall; it was too conspicuous.

It was a pretty river, bending and turning and flowing along in a quiet way. It wasn't Maine, but it was New England, and if they had to wait somewhere, this was a nice place. But it would be even nicer to move into their house. She said it aloud to Peter.

He stopped. "Prissy, you must not remember that house in Surrey very well."

"Of course I do." She remembered it vividly—the weathered gray clapboards, the central chimney, the hollyhocks all along the front of the house, the ocean across the road. Of course she remembered it.

"You were ten years old."

"So?"

"You only remember what you want to remember."

"I do not."

He closed one of his intensely blue eyes and squinted at her with the other one. "Do you remember how everybody huddles around the fireplaces because there's no central heating?"

"Are you so accustomed to central heating?"

"We've never stayed any place where we couldn't

keep warm. Even Finland. Especially Finland. And remember how they keep the snow off the roads in Finland? You never get snowbound. In Maine you get stuck all the time." He shook his head. "And that house. If we don't get there in time for Paul and me to rebuild it before winter, it just won't be livable."

"You're crazy. Grandfather lived there."

"He lived in the nursing home for two years before he died. That makes three years the place has been empty and who knows how many since any repairs were made. Do you remember the time Titania asked me to string a clothesline in that old parlor that was never used?"

"No."

"I put up the line, and when Titania hung up the clothes, the wall fell in." He laughed.

"You're making it up." But vaguely she did remember it.

"I am not. What a mess it was. Plaster, laths, wallpaper, dripping laundry. And Grandfather just looked at it and said, 'I had a notion that wall needed new plaster.'"

She laughed too. It sounded so like Grandfather. But surely a house that had stood for two hundred years could be restored. She came around a bend in the river and stopped short, unable to believe her eyes. "Peter, look!"

"Wow!" Peter stared. "If we were in Europe, I could believe it."

Set back from the river, on the edge of woods, was the unfinished facade of a castle, scaled down in size to fit the lot. The front, with a big arched entrance, was three stories high with an ornamental window set in the middle and slender spires at the top. The entrance was flanked by towers, one of them unfinished. Low stone walls curved away from the entrance. It looked like an ancient ruin or a bombed-out castle, now softened with ivy.

"Could it be a movie set?"

"No," Peter said, "with that ivy it's been here a long time." He ran up to the entrance and looked in. "Only one wing is even partly finished."

She followed him into what must have been meant to be an inner courtyard. On the right there was just a low, uneven wall of fieldstones, but on the left the wall had been completed on three sides, and the area had a roof and a stone floor. An enormous fireplace led to a big chimney. "Whatever could it be?"

"Maybe some rich American wanted his own castle and then died or went broke," Peter said.

"It looks enchanted."

"The great hall would have been about there," Peter said, squinting as if he were re-creating the castle in his mind.

"There would have been a beautiful circular staircase leading to the grand ballroom," Priscilla said. "There would have been a butler, and he would have announced us: 'Miss Priscilla Parkins and Mr. Peter Parkins of Surrey, Maine.'" She made a deep curtsy.

Peter smiled. "You live in the wrong century, Sis. You'd have wowed 'em as a lady-in-waiting or something."

"I'd have leaned out that balcony," she said, "the

one over the archway, and I'd have tossed a single red rose to my cavalier."

"That's what I don't dig. Why do you want so much to live in America? You're really romantic, but America isn't a romantic country."

"To me it is."

"I think you're in for a few cultural shocks." Peter loped off to the long wing. "Looks like they might have meant to put a kitchen in back here." He held up a length of copper pipe. "Perfectly good pipe, left lying around."

Priscilla half-closed her eyes and tried to picture the castle completed. A swirl of morning mist gave the unfinished walls a look of unreality. There was a birch and pine wood between the building and the road, so that the castle seemed quite cut off from the twentieth century. There was complete silence except for the whirr of grasshoppers and the hoarse caw of a crow, which flew low over their heads looking for a fence post to perch on.

"Let's tell Hazel," Priscilla said. "She'll love it."

But they had to wait to tell Hazel, because when they got back to the camping place, she was sitting cross-legged on the grass, meditating. The casket with the lodestone was in her lap. Priscilla had never seen the lodestone, nor had anyone except Hazel, as far as she knew. Hazel had found it in Addis Ababa just before Priscilla was born, and she had kept it ever since in the enameled box with the tiny silver padlock.

She had often told them the story of how she had found it. Some friends had driven them to a lake outside Addis Ababa. Things had been very bad for them;

they were out of money and Hazel had been expecting her second baby any minute. She felt very sick. So she sat on the shore of the lake, while the others went out in a boat. It got dark and she was worried and frightened. Suddenly an old woman, bent almost double, had appeared out of the darkness and spoken to her. Hazel hadn't understood her and grew more and more scared. The woman drew a small circle on the ground in front of Hazel, and then all at once she was gone, no sign of her at all. In a minute the moon rose, and Hazel saw a round stone in the center of the circle. It was a beautiful little stone and she had been sure it was not there before. She picked it up, and just then Paul and the others came back with a great catch of fish. They cooked some of it right there on the shore, and drank the wine their friends had brought, and everyone was suddenly happy. The next day Paul got a job on an excursion boat, and a week later Priscilla was born. As soon as she could, Hazel had gotten the beautiful little casket in the bazaar, and Paul had found her the silver padlock at a port on the Red Sea.

Whenever the family had problems or troubles, Hazel counted on the lodestone to tell her what to do. Peter and Priscilla had grown up believing in it, relying on the security it gave them. But one day, logic had struck Priscilla in the face like a dash of cold water. No little stone, no matter where or how you found it, could do anything for you. She had told Hazel it was as silly as believing in Santa Claus.

Hazel had looked at her sadly. "There are so many things, you know, that people believe in. Each of us has to decide which is his."

That had not seemed like any answer at all. She had tried to talk to Peter about it, but surprisingly he had refused to discuss it. Sometimes it almost seemed as if he still believed in it, a big seventeen-year-old boy like him. Priscilla tried mocking him, but he turned it off.

When Hazel had finished her meditation, they took her to see the skeleton castle. She looked at it with delight. "Who would have dreamed it?" she said. "Right here waiting for us. We have made the right moves."

Hazel always said things like that, which was one of the reasons Priscilla hoped she wouldn't get too friendly with the people in Surrey. They would accept a lot, but there were bound to be limits.

Peter, who was never thrown by anything Hazel said or did, took her around, showing her the place as if he were the lord of the manor. Priscilla sat on a boulder in front of the huge fireplace and watched them. They were a lot alike, Peter with shoulder-length wavy hair like Hazel's, tall and graceful like her, and with the kind of untouchable poise that Priscilla envied. Neither of them lost their temper or got flustered and worried the way Priscilla did. It was almost as if they moved in some other dimension. She sighed and got up to join them.

Three days later, when Paul came home in an old pickup to tell them that Puddleford had sold the camper, Hazel said serenely, "That's all right. Now we can move into the castle."

FOUR

JOURNAL: 15 August—in a town called South Naumkeag, Massachusetts, presently resident in a cow pasture (sans cows). 'Double, double, toil and trouble'! ! The part to fix the Fiat has to be sent overseas for. It will come by ship. Even if they shipped it the minute they got the order, which is unthinkable, it would take minimum six weeks to New York, plus a week to here, plus time to install, which brings us practically up to Christmas. The house in Surrey has not been fixed up for winter. Peter says they cannot fix it while there is six feet of snow and subzero temperatures. Last night Hazel and I slept in the tent on rocks, because this land is wall-to-wall rocks just like Finland. Peter and Paul slept in the open back of Mr. Puddleford's pickup. It rained. Everybody in bad mood this morning except, of course, Hazel, who is happy because she has problems to face. Hazel dives for trouble the way a hawk dives for an adder, but I would like to remind her that sometimes a hawk grabs a snake that sticks in his throat and then he is in real trouble. I cried half the night, but a soggy tent on a bed of rocks is not a comfortable place to cry. Sometimes I think and believe that Surrey and maybe the whole state of Maine is not a real place at all, but just a mirage that I dreamed up. Hazel has asked me to go with her to buy some eggs from Mrs. Puddleford. How does she know Mrs. Puddleford sells eggs? How does she know there is a Mrs. Puddleford? How does she know she won't sic the dog on us? He barks at night, and he sounds like the hound of the Baskervilles to me. Peter says I suffer from the Henry James syndrome. He says Henry James moaned a lot about how his parents bounced him all over Europe and America while he was growing up and he had no roots. I never read Henry James. Peter says I wouldn't understand him. I'd understand *that*. Peter says Henry James would not have been such a great writer if he hadn't had that kind of life. How does Peter know? If he's such a great writer, I suppose even a dope like me could understand him. If we're going to be stuck here, in this town, I might as well get a library card. Address: Puddleford's Cow Pasture.

F I V E

THE hound of the Baskervilles raised his voice as Priscilla and Hazel came up the weed-strewn driveway to the Puddleford house. Priscilla stopped as the big shaggy dog bounded around the corner of the house toward them. She liked dogs, but this one had a manner that made her cautious. Hazel didn't slow down at all.

"Good morning, dog," she said. She didn't hold out her hand or make soothing noises or anything. Just "Good morning, dog," and right on past him. The dog sniffed at her heels, growled a few times, and came toward Priscilla. Time and again Priscilla had seen Hazel use this technique with even the most formidable animals. It almost always worked. Peter said that was because an animal knows when you are scared or not. "Hazel isn't scared. They're fellow creatures."

"Scram, fellow creature," Priscilla said as the dog's cold nose touched her leg. "Scram. Don't take a hunk out of my leg."

Once Hazel's method hadn't worked. A Pekingese

in Stockholm had bitten her ankle. "It was because it was such a hot day," Hazel had said afterward, worrying about the dog. Hazel was unreal. Worrying about the dog while blood dripped from her ankle. In Finland, she was the only one of them who didn't walk in the middle of the road, pounding with a big stick to scare away the poisonous adders. Even the bent old women, who appeared out of the woods like ancient ghosts, carried sticks and beat the path. But not Hazel. "All creatures love Titania," Paul had said. "Foolhardy" was Priscilla's word for it.

Priscilla moved along the path because the dog was behind her. Hazel looked back and nodded approval. "That's right. He won't hurt you." She went up on the front step, which was a big granite millstone, and lifted the tarnished knocker and let it fall.

It was a long minute before the door was opened. A small, thin woman with straggly brown hair stood in the doorway looking at them with a little frown. She had on a frilled white apron over a pair of worn brown slacks. "If you're the new Avon lady," she said, "I told the other one, Pud don't like—"

"No, I'm not the Avon lady," Hazel said. "I'm Mrs. Parkins. My husband has gone to work for your husband."

The woman's face cleared. "Oh, you're them out in the pasture. Come in." She opened the door wider. Hazel and Priscilla went in. The dog sat on the millstone growling.

"Hush up your noise, Spot," Mrs. Puddleford said.

Priscilla glanced back at the dog before the heavy

old door closed. There was not a spot on him; his coat was all shaggy, dirty brown.

"Nobody hardly comes to the front door," Mrs. Puddleford said, "excepting Fuller Brush and Avon and like that. Come and sit." She took them into a long, low-ceilinged room with heavy beams running the length of the ceiling. One wall was a deep brick fireplace with a crane. There was a horsehair sofa and a matching rocker, an old bench, and a low armless Victorian chair covered with faded blue brocade. On the mahogany table there were several small daguerrotypes, and some more modern enlarged snapshots of what Priscilla assumed was Mr. and Mrs. Puddleford twenty years ago.

"What a fine old house you have," Hazel said.

Mrs. Puddleford shrugged. "It's a lot to look after. But it's been in Pud's family, you know. No sense hauling it down as long as it's sound. Hard as the dickens to heat, though. We shut off these front rooms in the cold weather." She looked at Hazel as if she had suddenly run out of things to say.

Very casually Hazel said, "That's an interesting old ruin over there in the field."

"Oh, that." Mrs. Puddleford sniffed contemptuously. "Them crazy Westons. A good thing he got put away before he finished it."

Priscilla leaned forward. "Is he in jail?" It was the first thing Priscilla had said, and Mrs. Puddleford glanced at her as if she were surprised to find her there.

"Oh, no. Not them Westons." She tapped her forehead. "Put away." And with sudden venom she said, "I hate the lot."

After a slight pause, Hazel said, "Not nice people," making it half a question, half a statement.

"Not what you'd call." Mrs. Puddleford's lip curled. "My dad was head steward at the club when it happened, you know."

Silence. Priscilla couldn't stand it. "What happened?" She caught, out of the corner of her eye, Hazel's frown—meaning don't pry.

"Oh, you know. When the old man Weston, father of the one that's put away—and the old man should have been put away too in the opinion of many—rode right up to Pud's father and conked him over the head with his mallet."

"How did he ever come to do such a wicked thing?" Hazel asked.

"Well, it was a bitter game, you know. Those polo matches were out for blood. Old Mr. Puddleford got in a stroke ahead of him. Old Weston always did have a sinful temper, you know."

"Did it kill Mr. Puddleford's father?" Priscilla asked.

"Might as well have. Poor old man never came back to his real senses, and of course he was blind in that eye."

"He should have sued him," Priscilla said. Her grandfather used to talk about suing people he thought had done him an injustice.

"Oh, he did. But what's the good of suing a Weston?" She smoothed her apron. "But now they caught up with the young one, the good Lord and his angels. He's shut up, hopeless. Wife dead, children dead. Nobody left but that cousin in Italy, and it's a cinch she don't want that crazy monstrosity over there." She gestured toward the meadow. "The Lord moves in mysterious ways, dearie."

"Indeed yes," Hazel said. "Will they sell the place, then?"

"Can't. Not yet a while. It's all tied up. Well, it just sits there, and nobody ever goes near it. It don't hurt, I guess."

Hazel rose. She was wearing the long black skirt with the embroidered red roses that she had made, and one of Paul's T-shirts. "I was wondering, Mrs. Puddleford, if we could buy a few of your nice fresh eggs."

"Sure." Mrs. Puddleford got up and led them down a narrow hall to the big kitchen. "Kath," she called in a suddenly shrill voice, "get the folks some eggs."

The girl in cut-offs whom Priscilla and Peter had seen feeding the chickens stuck her head in the door. "How many?" She was sixteen or seventeen, broad like her father but not yet fat. She looked at Hazel and Priscilla with more curiosity than her mother had.

"Oh, a dozen," Mrs. Puddleford said. "Dozen or so." When the girl disappeared, she added, "Like a cup of coffee?" She had three pies set out on the counter, ready for baking. Priscilla could hardly remember what an American pie tasted like, except that it was delicious.

Hazel declined the coffee with thanks, paid for the eggs, and invited Mrs. Puddleford to come and call. Priscilla blinked. "Do sit down, Mrs. Puddleford," she thought, "here on this comfy rock."

As she saw them to the door, Mrs. Puddleford said, "Pud says you been across the water."

"Yes," Hazel said, "we've spent most of our married life in Europe."

"My dad come from over that way," Mrs. Puddleford said. "Yorkshire."

"Oh yes. Remember Yorkshire, Prissy?"

Priscilla didn't, not really.

"Pud nor I got no desire to cross the water," Mrs. Puddleford said. "No desire." She folded her thin arms and watched them go down the driveway, but when Priscilla turned back, she had already gone inside.

"We can start moving in," Hazel said.

"Move in where?" For a minute Priscila thought her mother meant move in with the Puddlefords.

Hazel looked surprised. "Why, the castle, dear." She smiled a secret, happy smile. "I've always wanted to live in a castle."

"So have I," Priscilla said, "but not in a cow pasture."

"Priscilla dear," Hazel said, "you must learn in life to take your castles where you find them."

S I X

T HE whole family went to town with Paul in the morning, Peter and Priscilla huddled up in the back of the dirty little truck. Peter had an appointment with the druggist about a part-time job. His brown hair was neatly combed, and he was wearing his best white shirt.

"Hey," he said to Priscilla, "don't I look like a real American boy?"

"You are a real American boy, stupid."

Priscilla hadn't wanted to go to town, but Hazel wanted her to come. Priscilla dreaded walking around this town they were going to live in. She was afraid the people wouldn't like the Parkinses. She had put on clean jeans and a turtleneck sweater that she'd bought in a discount store outside Boston. After she had snapped at Peter, it occurred to her that she, too was trying to look like an American. That's what came of living all over the place instead of where you belonged. You didn't know who you were. It would be good to settle down in the USA and not have to make adjustments all the time to strange languages, strange customs.

She looked at her mother to see how she would strike the Yankees. Would they think she was weird? Hazel was wearing a long, full peasant skirt from Norway and a square-necked embroidered blouse.

When she saw Priscilla looking at her, she said, "I'm wearing the dark skirt, dear." She meant, "so you won't be ashamed of me."

Priscilla sighed. What could you do with a mother that thought a skirt was conservative just because it was dark blue? It was covered with bright yellow, red, and blue embroidered flowers; it was full enough for a tent; and it came about four inches above the ankles.

Hazel had braided her hair and put it around her head like a coronet. She was wearing the reindeer shoes from Lapland, with the toes that curled up like the front of a toboggan.

"You look pretty, Ma," Peter said, when she got out of the car at the garage.

"Thank you, dear," she said. "My children look very handsome this morning, very American." She kissed Paul. "See you later." She took Peter and Priscilla across the street to the Paper Store for a cup of coffee at the long counter. The unsmiling woman who swished a rag along the counter in front of them looked sharply at Hazel. "What's yours?" she muttered.

"*Kahvia*," Hazel said, and then as Priscilla gave her a fierce nudge, she corrected herself: "Coffee, please. What do you want, children?"

"*Kahvia.*" Peter grinned at Priscilla's embarrassment at their lapse into Finnish.

"I'd like a glass of milk," she said, louder than necessary.

"One coffee, one milk . . . what's for him?" The woman looked at them suspiciously.

"He wants coffee, too." Hazel got up and got a copy of the Boston *Globe* and turned to the astrology column. She folded the paper neatly and studied the predictions for all four of them, herself the Aquarian, Paul the Pisces, Peter the Virgo, and Priscilla the Capricorn.

"You'll get your job, dear," she said to Peter.

He nodded. "I thought I would."

"Paul will have a good day. I will make some discoveries; well, I intended to. Capricorn, people close to you will make you impatient, but try to be understanding; they think well of you." Hazel looked up and saw the woman scowling at her. "What's your sign, dear?"

The woman sniffed. "That's just a bunch of witchcraft."

"Well, not really." Hazel's voice was explaining rather than arguing. "Witchcraft is really quite different. Witchcraft involves—"

"Mother!" Hazel looked at her; she knew Priscilla was upset when she called her "mother."

"Yes, Prissy?"

"Please pass the sugar."

Peter laughed. "For your milk, Sis?"

"For your coffee, stupid."

"You know I don't take sugar."

"Hush," Hazel said. "Don't argue. Don't call your brother 'stupid.' It's degrading."

But the diversion had worked. The scowling woman had moved away, sloshing dirty dishes in a sink at the end of the counter.

Hazel looked disappointed. "I wanted to explain to her . . . So many people don't understand—"

The door was pushed open and a woman strode in. She was a stocky, broad-shouldered woman, in tan riding pants and knee-high polished boots, a pale blue silk shirt, and a dark blue beret. She picked up a paper, and since the man at the counter was in the back of the store, she brought a dollar to the counter. "Will you get me change, Myrt?" she said, in a strong voice. "I've got a *Globe*."

"Sure thing." The waitress' face looked different when she smiled.

While she waited for her change, the woman in the riding pants glanced at Hazel's paper. "How does it look for Aries?"

Hazel gave her a quick smile and read it to her. "You will have a change of plans. Keep your bags packed. The new itinerary will irk you at first, but later you will be pleased."

"Oh, blast!" the woman said. "I don't want to change my plans." She took her change from the waitress. To Hazel she said, "Beautiful skirt. Scandinavian, isn't it?"

"Yes, Norwegian."

"Lovely." She looked as if she'd like to say more but a horn blew outside. She smiled at them. "Cheerio."

Peter jumped up and opened the door for her.

She said, "Thank you, young man."

"Not at all. Is the Rover running all right?"

She looked surprised. "Some nice young man who knows about English cars—" She interrupted herself, pointing at him. "Your father?"

Peter grinned. "Yes, Mrs. Wentworth."

"Oh, lovely." She looked back at Hazel. "I understand you've traveled a great deal. We must talk sometime—" She broke off as the horn sounded again. "My impatient child. Sorry." She hurried out.

The waitress was more cordial. "That's a great lady," she said.

"Yes," Hazel said. "I knew right away she was Aries."

The woman gave her a long, careful look. "You Paul's bunch?"

"I'm Paul's wife. These are our children."

It often seemed to Priscilla that Hazel didn't even know it when someone was insulting her or being obnoxious. But as Peter said, whether she knew it or not, she always answered with so much dignity that if a person did mean to be insulting, it fell flat.

"He comes in for coffee," the waitress said. "Nice guy, for a hippie."

Peter gave her a friendly smile. "We aren't hippies. Hippies are out of style."

She shrugged. "I wouldn't know. Beatniks, maybe."

Peter laughed. "Beatniks were out before I was born. My dad belonged to the Young Socialist League when he was in theology school. I guess they're gone down the drain, too."

"In my dad's day, it was Bohemians," Hazel said.

"He was a Bohemian in Greenwich Village once, a Bohemian from Council Bluffs, Iowa."

"I seen Greenwich Village," the waitress said. "I was down to New York once with my old man, to the World's Fair." She leaned her elbows on the counter and stared into her memories.

"That woman was sure crabby," Priscilla said when they left, "till that Mrs. Wentworth spoke to us." They were outside now and the town was slowly coming to life.

Hazel shook her head. "It's hard to overflow with the milk of human kindness when you have to get up at dawn to shovel out stale doughnuts and bad coffee. And nothing to dream about but the World's Fair. I was a waitress once."

Peter went along to the drugstore for his interview after they had wandered up and down the street inspecting the various stores. Hazel and Priscilla stopped in the car lot to get Hazel's comb from the Fiat's pocket.

Priscilla patted the bright red door. "Get well quick, Fiat."

Hazel looked at her. "I'm sorry we didn't get you to Surrey, Pris. I know how disappointed you are. You've been a good sport."

"We'll get there." It embarrassed Priscilla for her mother to praise her, because in her heart she had not been a good sport at all.

"Yes, you Capricorns usually get where you're going." She paused as they came back to the sidewalk. "Only sometimes I think you're so engrossed in the business of getting there, you forgot to take a good look at where it is you're going. Surrey really isn't any-body's dream world."

"It's mine."

Hazel said no more. They walked around the corner where the drugstore stood but Priscilla couldn't see any sign of Peter. Across the wide square a silver two-car train glided silently into the station, and several men with briefcases got on. A Volvo station wagon raced up to the tracks and stopped with a squeal. A young man flung open the door and ran for the train. He jumped for the steps of the last car and just made it. Laughing and waving, he hung to the handrail. The young woman in the car waved and slid into the driver's seat and roared off.

Hazel laughed. "He must be a lawyer or the owner of the business or something. The wage slaves went in an hour ago."

For a moment Priscilla envied the young woman in the Volvo. If anything happened, like Surrey being wiped off the map, maybe she'd like to stay here and be married to a suburbanite like that. She'd get him to the train on time and meet him at night, and during the day she'd garden and cook and do cryptograms. And read the news so she could discuss his work in-telligently.

"Look." Hazel pointed to the window of a dusty, cluttered little store whose sign said JESSIE'S DRY GOODS. The window displayed limp rayon blouses, boys' pants, some drab scarves, half a dozen dead flies, and three hand-lettered and decorated signs. One sign had a large, slightly lopsided figure of a telephone dial, and in the middle it said: DIAL A PRAYER, AND THEN

CALL JESSIE FOR BARGAINS. A smaller sign said: SOLVE YOUR OWN PROBLEMS: GOD HAS OTHER THINGS TO DO. And the third one said: GOD HATETH A DRUNKARD, and there was an elaborate arrow pointing toward the beer parlor next door.

Hazel whipped a piece of paper and a pencil out of her big leather purse. She braced the paper on the streaked glass and printed in large letters: IN SOME PLACES GOD HAS TO HAVE MORE PATIENCE THAN IN OTHERS. And before Priscilla could believe what she was doing, she went inside the store.

Priscilla followed her. The woman behind the counter gave them a broad smile. She was short, about the same width in all of her that Priscilla could see. She had a gold tooth that flashed in the dim store. Her coarse gray hair was cut short.

"Morning. Help you?" Her voice was loud. She looked them over with shrewd eyes and her manner turned patronizing. "If you just want to look—"

"I was interested in the signs in your window," Hazel said sweetly. She held out her own. "I wrote another one."

The woman glanced at it without much interest and handed it back. "Put it in the window if you want to. It's a good thought. I like philosophy. Put it next to the church supper sign."

Priscilla suddenly felt as if she had to say something. "There isn't any church supper sign."

The woman wasn't paying any further attention to them. "Oh, I must have pulled it out. Well, just drop it in there."

Hazel placed it carefully in a conspicuous place. Just

as they were leaving, the woman's brassy voice called after them. "What group you with?"

"Group?" Hazel said.

"What religious bunch? Are you Jesus people? I don't hold with Jesus people."

"We belong to the Parkins Believers," Hazel said, and walked out.

As she followed her mother, Priscilla heard the woman say, "That's a new one on me."

SEVEN

Since Paul had not yet been paid, they had very
little money, but Hazel wanted to get what she
called the lay of the land. She bought some
postcards at the drugstore and some overseas stamps at
the post office.

They stopped at a small Greek delicatessen. The
proprietor, a small skinny man, put his hands on his
hips and looked at Hazel with amusement when she
asked for herb tea.

"Lady, I got no herbs, no simples. Just plain old
English breakfast, oolong, orange pekoe. What you
want with herb tea? You a nutrition nut?" He winked
at a man who was picking up groceries.

"I'll take some English breakfast," Hazel said
serenely.

"Or a witch maybe?" The man laughed. "Going to
brew a little something, eh? I mean, with those
shoes . . . Lady, where did you get those shoes?"

Angrily, Priscilla slammed some money down on the
counter. "Could my mother just have her purchase if

you please," she said in her stoniest voice, "without comments?" She was afraid of Yankees, but shopkeepers like this she knew about.

The Greek man shrugged, laughed, and put the tea in a bag. He said something rapidly in Greek and winked again at the other man.

Hazel said "Thank you and good-bye" in Greek and they left the store, the man staring after them.

"What was he saying?"

Hazel laughed. "All I know in Greek is 'hello,' 'how are you?' 'thank you,' 'how much,' and 'good-bye.' "

"We're getting off to a great start. You insulted dry goods and I snarled at delicatessen."

"Delicatessen needed snarling at and will respect us for it. Dry goods doesn't know she was insulted." They walked along the main road, the portion of Route 1A that ran through the town. They passed once substantial late nineteenth- and early twentieth-century houses, now in some cases gone to seed, or in other cases converted to real estate offices, a travel bureau, a garage and gas station.

They had just come to an attractive brick building called South Naumkeag Community House, when a small panel truck that said CONWAY DRUG slued to a stop beside them in a shower of gravel. Peter beamed at them.

"Got the job! I'm delivering prescriptions already. Make way for the messenger bearing life-healing drugs. Make way for the messenger from Garcia!" He gunned the engine.

"Wonderful!" Hazel called to him. And as he

started up, she shouted, "Darling, don't drive like a Finn."

"I wonder how much he'll get paid," Priscilla said, as the little truck sped off.

"That's not important. It's good for him to have a job; good for his self-confidence."

It had never occurred to Priscilla that Peter was in any crying need of self-confidence. They walked on past the playground, past the library, which wasn't open yet, and past the high school.

"We'll have to talk to them," Hazel said, looking at the school.

"Not today, please." Priscilla didn't feel up to that yet.

They passed a polo field and a sign that pointed down a dirt lane to the Hunt Club.

"I hope it's not real foxes," Hazel said.

Priscilla hoped so too. She remembered the little village in England that her mother had thrown into tumult in her defense of the fox against the historic right of the English hunter.

The elms and maples lined the road they now walked, making a leafy arch. On either side of the road they saw large, gracious houses with long driveways leading to them. Many had stables and horses grazing in paddocks.

"This must be a town the wealthy Bostonians fled to," Hazel said.

Instead of marrying a commuting lawyer, perhaps, Priscilla thought, she would fall in love with the heir to one of these beautiful homes. She would ride to the hounds and serve tea every afternoon and take two borzois with her wherever she went. She would become known as the Lady of the Borzois.

They sat down to rest on a stone wall that was draped with sumac. Priscilla had been disappointed not to find stone walls in Surrey. She had assumed they were everywhere in New England.

When they moved on again, they passed a sign on a piece of weathered board that said R. W. WENT-WORTH. Priscilla tried to see the house, but it was hidden beyond a winding road.

They came to the Town Hall, which was Hazel's goal. It was a big white neo-Greek building with a small gilt dome. Across the street was a village green with two very old saltbox-type houses and a beautiful, little white steepled church.

"Oh, how nice," Priscilla said. This looked the way it ought to.

"This is the original town. The other part grew up around the railroad station."

"How do you know?"

"Paul said so." She led the way up the steps into the Town Hall.

"Now what?" Priscilla said, but Hazel didn't answer.

Instead she went to a door that said TOWN CLERK. It was open. Hazel knocked lightly and stepped in. Behind a big desk, with file cabinets at his back, sat a tall, broad-shouldered man in a white shirt and a tie, with glasses that slid down his narrow nose. He looked at them as they came in.

"Morning."

"Good morning. Excuse me for bothering you . . ."

"Not at all."

"I'm awfully interested in the beautiful old houses you have in this town. I wondered if you had any booklet about them, or something of that sort."

The man opened a drawer and shuffled through some papers. "Had one here somewhere. The Historical Society people put one out . . ." He pulled out a handful of brochures. "Got it here somewhere." He gave Priscilla a quick grin. "I need a secretary, don't I, young lady."

She smiled, not sure what she should say, but more than that, concerned with what Hazel was up to. She waited a minute, listening to Hazel commenting on the two houses across the street, and the Town Clerk telling her their dates: then she slipped out into the hall and looked around. There were signs over the various doors: TAX COLLECTOR; ASSESSOR; POLICE; BOARD OF SELECTMEN. Across the hall on an old door with small windows, some metal letters had been removed, leaving the faded outline of the word LIBRARY. She tried to look in but the room was dark.

When she came back to the Town Clerk's office, Hazel was sitting down, with a booklet open in her lap, talking with the man.

"That ruin out on Willow Lane," she said. "That must be quite old."

He laughed. "About thirty years. Mr. Weston was planning a real castle, a slightly smaller version of Henry the Eighth's little love nest—"

"Hampton Court," Hazel said.

"I believe so." He looked impressed. "It was to have a maze, as I understand it, like that place?"

"Yes. How fascinating. Hampton Court is red brick, though, and he used fieldstones—Mr. Weston, I mean."

"Yes, handier, I guess, and more impressive around here."

"I wonder if he meant to have a deer park."

The Town Clerk laughed. "Probably. Though there's not all that much land. Or deer, unless he imported them—which he was capable of. And rich enough to do."

"What happened?"

She's leading him on, Priscilla thought; she knows what happened. Although it was true she had already picked up some new information. Henry the Eighth yet!

"Poor guy lost his mind. He's been in a hospital for twenty-five years. His wife and children were killed in a train wreck. The estate is all tied up. His cousin will get it when he dies, I guess. She pays the taxes, just to be sure." He chuckled. "Although she spits like a tomcat every time she gets the bill. She sent Bernie a cable last time—Bernie's the tax collector."

"She's in Europe?"

"Yes. She was living in Florence . . . guess she still is. She's gone through a couple of counts and a millionaire or two, but she's always pleading poverty." He tipped his chair back. "I talk too much."

"But it's so interesting."

"Well, it's all common knowledge."

"What is her name? We know people in Florence . . ."

"I think the latest name is Mrs. Jonathan Wilder, but Mr. W. long since flew the coop."

Hazel got up. "Well, I mustn't keep you. But such a fascinating story! I wonder if Mrs. Wilder will ever sell . . ."

Priscilla almost laughed. Was Hazel trying to make him think she'd like to buy?

"Who knows. She's unpredictable. The place would have to be torn down of course, but the land is valuable."

"What is the tax rate? What would taxes on a piece of land like that be?"

He picked up the phone and pushed a button. Priscilla heard a phone ring down the hall.

"Bernie, what are the taxes on the Weston place?" He held the phone to his chest. "He'll look it up."

"Oh, I didn't mean to bother him. I was just curious."

"No bother." He spoke into the phone. "Yeah, Bernie. Thanks."

"It'll take him a minute. If you want to stop by his office, right next door . . ."

"Thank you so much." Hazel held out her hand. "You've been very kind to an inquisitive stranger."

He smiled. "Glad to have you folks among us. Hope you like us." He nodded pleasantly to Priscilla. "Enjoy yourself, young lady."

They went to the smaller office next door, and a small man who was going through an ancient-looking file nodded. "Have it right here, madam."

"It's very good of you." Hazel sat on a bench.

They think she's going to buy a lot of land, Priscilla

thought. They think she's an eccentric rich woman. She wasn't sure whether the idea horrified her or amused her. It *was* funny.

"Here we are." The man straightened up. "Last year she paid $1,150. Might go up a bit this year. Like everything else. Wicked, isn't it, the way prices go up."

"They do seem high," Hazel said. She was writing down $1,150 on a slip of paper. "We've been in Europe a long time so it's hard to compare."

He looked impressed. "Been in Europe, have you? Like it over there?"

"Yes, we enjoy it."

"But there's no place like the good old USA, I guess."

"That's what my daughter says." Hazel smiled at Priscilla. "She's a great fan of the USA."

It was a weird way to put it, Priscilla thought, as if they were discussing cricket teams. Or baseball. Forget cricket.

The man tapped the file. "That's where *she* lives, you know. Europe. Sally Weston." With mockery he said, "Mrs. Jonathan Wilder this week, I believe. Who knows what next week."

"Yes. I believe Mr. Whipple said she lives in Florence?"

"Not now. She's in that little country"—he checked the paper in front of him—"Liechtenstein. Place called V-a-d-u-z."

"Vaduz, oh yes. I love Liechtenstein. Well, thank you very much, Mr." Hazel glanced at the brass nameplate on his desk—"Mr. Haskell."

"My pleasure. You folks living here now?"

"Right at the moment we're just camping out," she said, "near Mr. Puddleford's house. My husband is working for Mr. Puddleford."

Mr. Haskell looked surprised. "Oh, sure. Well, it'll be getting chilly for camping out."

"Yes. Thank you again." Hazel gave him a brilliant smile and they left.

Mr. Whipple met them in the hall. "If you'd like to take a look at some of the old town histories, we keep them in here." He unlocked the door to the room that said LIBRARY. "Used to be the town library before we got our new one." He opened the door and turned on the light.

"Gosh," Priscilla said softly. There were rows and rows of old leatherbound books.

"I have some errands that need doing," Hazel said, "but if I could leave my daughter here for a while? And I'd like to come and look at them later myself, if I could?"

"Sure thing. Just let me know when you leave so I can lock up." He went back to his office.

"I'll see you here later," Hazel said, and she was gone almost before Priscilla noticed.

She began with a brown leatherbound book titled "NAUMKEAG: Being the Historie of the Settlement and Its Becoming a Township, Up To Anno Dominie 1782." For more than an hour she read not only the early history of the town but its lists of inhabitants, tax lists, births and deaths. Almost at the end of the book, in the year 1781, she came across a Parkins. Amos Parkins had married Annie Francis. A Parkins! She looked up, dazed from reading, and watched dust specks dancing in the stream of sunlight that came in the many-paned window. A Parkins in Naumkeag. It must be a sign.

E I G H T

J OURNAL: 29 August—I have here a copy of the
letter composed by my mother and mailed *par
avion* by my father, addressed to Mrs. Jonathan
Wilder, c / o Peter Lydman, National Tourist Office,
Vaduz, Liechtenstein. 'My dear Mrs. Wilder: I beg to
introduce myself and my family. We are of the Parkins family of Maine, in late years residents of Europe
[Note by P.P.: insert 'Surrey' before 'Maine']. Coming to the States after so many years abroad, we chance
to find ourselves in the charming town of South
Naumkeag, Mass. Understandably enchanted with the
fine castle begun by your family—intended, we understand, to be a replica on smaller scale of Hampton
Court—we would like to ask your kind permission to
rent from you that portion which is partially habitable,
and which my husband, who is gifted in that direction, would make even more habitable. We find here
such excellent vibrations [note by P.P.: 'vibrations'
crossed out, 'ambience' substituted], which reminds
us of England. Until there is time for the, oh, so slow

55

overseas mail to confirm, I am taking the liberty of sending you a check for $75, trusting this will seem to you adequate as a monthly rate [note by P.P.: cross out 'rate,' substitute 'rent'; cross out 'rent,' replace 'rate'] for your property, which must otherwise be such a tax drain for you. You are sure to know our good friend Peter Lydman, who will, I am confident, vouch for us [note by P.P.: cross out 'I am confident']. And you may also know dear Harry Wetherby, whose art gallery is so well known in Florence, where we understand you recently resided. Until we hear from you, my dear Mrs. Wilder, rest assured we will proceed with all care for your fascinating property. We shall indeed guard it as if it were our own. Respectfully yours, Titania Parkins.'

What I said was, "It's illegal." And Paul said, "But so imaginative!" And Peter said, "It sounds as if it were written by Jane Austen and translated into a foreign language and translated back in English by someone whose native language is not English." I had to laugh at that, because it does. Hazel said she meant it to sound continental. The whole scheme is insane, and we will probably end up in jail. What a way to start our return to our native land. It's a blasted good thing they don't still have the stocks to punish people. I can picture the four Parkinses down in the square with their hands and feet stuck through holes in hunks of wood, and the dry goods woman and the Greek delicatessen throwing buttons and ripe tomatoes at us. Why, oh why, oh why can't we lead a NORMAL life??!!

I told Paul about the Parkins in Naumkeag. He

didn't seem overcome by the news. "If you go back far enough," he said, "everybody's related."

He gets paid tomorrow. He and Peter are going to the lumber yard to buy the fourth wall for our castle. We have already begun to move in. The fireplace works. I begin to get this peculiar feeling that I am Anne Boleyn.

NINE

ON the Sunday afternoon when the last section of wall slid into place between the supporting stone pillars, the sun broke through a gray sky for the first time in a week. Hazel and Priscilla stood back and cheered. For days and days they had all thought of nothing but getting the house finished. They were tired, especially Paul, who had worked every night after he got home from the garage. To make the most of daylight, he had never stopped to eat more than a quick sandwich until it was too dark to work. Then he would eat something hot and read a chapter in one of his philosophy books until, as he said, his muscles unkinked enough so he could sleep.

He stretched now and smiled at Hazel. "Home sweet home."

"It's beautiful." Hazel put her arm around him.

Paul and Peter had built the wall of board-and-batten, sprayed with a weathered gray stain that blended well with the stone.

"A little moss," Peter said, "a little ivy, and it'll

look as old as Hampton Court." He pushed his hair back from his face, leaving a streak of paint on his cheek. "We're guardians of the ghosts of Henry the Eighth, Katherine of Aragon, the whole lot."

Priscilla laughed nervously. Normal ghosts might not be too scary but she didn't think she wanted to encounter any beheaded ones. "It's a good thing there really aren't any ghosts."

Hazel smiled. "You rational Capricorns."

"Paul, you can do anything, can't you," Priscilla said, as much to change the subject as to tell her father she admired his skill.

Paul looked pleased. "Thanks to the *Whole Earth* catalog."

He had installed a small bathroom with a shower, connecting it to the sewer that was already there. He had put in a kitchen sink, too, connecting the pipes to the well. The pipes strewn in a heap of rubble were good copper pipes, still usable. The well was run by a small built-in generator which, to everyone's surprise, worked after a little fixing.

He and Peter had partitioned the huge room with beaverboard panels to make a large living room around the fireplace, a small kitchen, and three small bedrooms. The floor had already been paved with flagstones. Hazel put up her favorite Finnish hanging, woven in bright colors. In the woods she had found a copper kettle crusted over with thick black soot and dirt, and when she finally got it clean, she planted ferns in it and set it by the door that Paul had bought cheap at the lumber yard because it was an odd size.

Electricity—except for the small generator and mo-

tor that ran the pump—would have to wait, because
Paul would need a permit, and he was not anxious to
call attention to what they were doing. But they were
used to Coleman lanterns, and Hazel found a pretty
kerosine lamp in a secondhand store for two dollars.

It had been one of Priscilla's jobs to cut out foam-
rubber seats for the rocks and stumps that Hazel's odd
bits of material—which she always saved—transformed
into attractive, comfortable chairs. Peter made a dining table out of another door and supporting stumps,
and Paul was working on dining chairs. Bookshelves
had already gone up and were filled. In the evenings,
Paul also worked on frames for beds. Until they were
finished, they slept in their sleeping bags on the hard
flagstones.

For Priscilla it had been an exciting time, because
it was the first home of their own that they had had
in years. They were not nomads anymore; they were
New England settlers, with overtones of Henry the
Eighth. It wasn't Surrey, but it would do until Surrey
became possible.

The main thing she had to worry about was whether
someone would discover them and throw them out.
Her mother said they would be all right because she
had paid rent to Mrs. Wilder; but anyone but Hazel
would stop to think that you had to have the owner's
permission to rent, and a receipt and all that. No one
ever seemed to come near the castle, although Priscilla
wondered if the Puddlefords could hear the hammer-
ing; they were not far away. Mr. Puddleford seemed
to assume that they were still camping in his pasture,
but surely when it got cold and snowed, he would in-

quire. Paul said he might wonder but he would probably not mention it, because he had the kind of mind that preferred to ignore problems, hoping they would then disappear. In a town where there was almost nothing to rent, he would not want to worry about where Paul was going to live.

The night after the walls went up, Priscilla snuggled up in her sleeping bag, watching the shadows from the fire flickering on the ceiling until she fell asleep.

She awoke some time later, frightened. She had been dreaming that Anne Boleyn was knocking at the gate, crying to be let in. In the dream Priscilla had been afraid to let her in because she knew she had already been beheaded. She lay still, shivering. The house was quiet. From the next room she could hear Peter's breathing. She wriggled further down into the sleeping bag and closed her eyes. But there was the knocking again. It was real! She lay very still. It wasn't like an ordinary knock by a real person; it was a very quick *knock-knock-pause, knock-knock-pause, knock-knock-knock*. It was not loud, but it was insistent.

Frightened, she unzipped the sleeping bag and got up. No sense trying to wake Peter; that took at least fifteen minutes, and then he woke up with such loud confusion and alarm, he'd scare off whoever had knocked. She wanted the knocker to go away, but she also wanted to see who or what it was. She was very scared, but her mind ordered her to find an explanation. She hesitated in front of the curtain that closed off Hazel's and Paul's room. It wasn't right to wake Paul; he was so tired.

The knocking changed to a different rhythm, still

very rapid. It seemed to be at the front door. She slid along the wall until she came to one of the windows that still had no glass in it. She wanted to put her head out and look, but she didn't dare. It would be better to fling open the door and take whoever it was by surprise. If she had the nerve. There was bright moonlight, so she would be able to see. It rather surprised her that a ghost would come as close to dawn as she now saw it was; she would have expected midnight in a thick fog. Then she tried to remind herself that she did not, of course, believe in ghosts. And as she reached for the door, the thought struck her that the knocker might be even more frightening than a ghost. But there was no time to hesitate. She flung the door open.

No one was there. After she made sure of it, she stepped outside. There was no one, but the knocking had not stopped. It was not at the door at all. But where, then?

She stepped in what seemed to be the right direction, a little beyond the house, somewhere among the woods that separated the castle from Willow Lane. Suddenly she jumped. She thought she screamed but she heard nothing. A tall, shadowy figure was coming toward her from the woods. She turned to run back to the house.

"Priscilla, wait."

The voice was soft, and for a moment she was too stunned with fear to recognize it. But the figure came closer. It was Paul. With a little sob of relief she ran and threw her arms around him. He held her tight.

"I'm sorry I scared you, honey. I didn't know you were here."

The knocking had not stopped.

"What is it?" She still clung to him.

"That's what I came out to see. Come on, I'll show you. Nothing to be afraid of." He took her hand and led her a little way into the woods. In a small clearing there stood a tall telephone pole. Paul pointed to the top. At first she couldn't see anything, but then she saw the woodpecker, working away at the top of the pole, too busy to notice them. His black and white feathers reminded her of a speckled hen she'd been fond of once in Austria. She leaned against her father in relief.

"I was so scared."

"You were brave to come out alone but kind of foolish. Next time call one of us." They walked toward the house.

"I thought if it was one of Henry's wives with her head cut off, I'd just as soon not see her." Priscilla laughed nervously. "But there aren't any ghosts, are there?"

"Henry and his wives were never here, you see, so they have no reason to haunt an American place."

She persisted. "But there aren't any ghosts, are there?" She knew he wouldn't laugh at her. He never did.

"I'm not absolutely sure what is meant by ghosts," he said, "and I don't know what I believe. The older I get, the more I think all things are possible." He followed her into the dark living room. "The Church of England recently appointed an official head exorcist, you know."

"What does an exorcist do?"

"Drives out demons, evil spirits."

She shivered. "I wish everything was clear. I mean like you could ask questions and get the right answers."

"We all wish that."

She thought of the nights he sat up late reading books on philosophy and theology. She had never realized before that it was his search for answers.

When he'd gone into bed, Priscilla heard Hazel say sleepily, "What was it?"

"A woodpecker," he said.

TEN

Paul decreed that Labor Day would be their day for fun. In all the hurry of getting the house done, Priscilla and Peter had not yet registered for school. They would have to do that on Tuesday because school opened on Wednesday. But on Labor Day no one was to think of anything but having a good time.

Hazel packed one of her enormous picnic baskets. In the morning they all piled into Mr. Puddleford's old pickup, which he let Paul keep all the time now, and Paul drove them to the Hunt Club to watch the Labor Day polo game. He parked the pickup with its front wheels almost touching the thin, foot-high white wooden fence that bordered the polo field. On their left there was a late-model MG, with a handsome young man and a beautiful girl in it. While Peter muttered his admiration of the MG, Priscilla silently appreciated the young man and the girl. He had his arm along the back of the seat, and she kept looking at him with obvious adoration. They both wore white tennis shorts and white button-down, short-sleeved shirts, almost like a brother and sister outfit. Except they were obviously not brother and sister.

Priscilla's enjoyment of them was shattered when the girl looked at the pickup, and at Hazel, in her voluminous Norwegian skirt and her square-necked blouse and with the eight silver bracelets and the floppy hat. The girl said something to the boy; he looked, and they both laughed. Priscilla hated them.

On the field a young man in white riding pants and a scarlet and white silk shirt and a white polo helmet rode his horse up and down the field, cantering right up to the goalposts and then stopping suddenly and swerving. It was a beautiful bay horse, trained to the precision of a ballet dancer. Priscilla watched, fascinated. Other players were beginning to ride out to the field.

Paul brought containers of coffee for Hazel and himself and hot dogs for Priscilla and Peter. Hazel shook her head at the hot dogs. "Do we have to get all that American?" She disapproved of processed food. She liked to collect weeds and herbs and cook them in surprising and often delicious ways. She had already found many edible things growing along the river by the castle.

The players began to group themselves in opposing teams on the field. A tall, thin man with a receding chin rode in among them with the big white wooden ball.

"That guy on the bay is Hollister Wentworth," Peter said. "Mrs. Wentworth's son."

Priscilla flushed, as if Peter had noticed her admiration. "How do you know?"

"He came in for the Rover. There's a girl too, named Anne. They're nice."

The game began with surprising suddenness. All at once the horses were in motion, crowding each other, wheeling, stopping, leaping forward, turning in space that seemed too small to turn in. The loud whack of mallets against ball and mallets striking each other, and the whistling breath of the horses were the only sounds, except now and then a groan from the crowd at a stroke missed, or a low cheer at a goal. It was all very fast and exciting. Priscilla sometimes lost track of the ball altogether. She held her breath every time Hollister Wentworth hit the ball, and that seemed quite often. His tanned face under the white visor of his helmet was tight with concentration. He seemed to her to ride better than any of them, and surely his horse was more beautiful than the others. He was like some magnificent knight. He never once looked at the spectators. He seemed to exist in a world apart, even during the breaks in the game.

It was a crisp early fall day, sunny and a little windy but warm. Behind them on the porch of the low, graceful clubhouse, which Paul said was a hundred years old, people sat at little tables and drank coffee. Others swam and splashed in the pool. The tennis courts were full.

"It looks English," Hazel said. "It makes me nostalgic."

People rode around the outside of the field on their own horses, and once Priscilla caught sight of Mrs.

Wentworth sitting solidly astride a big black hunter. She looked at her with new interest, as the mother of Hollister.

All too soon the first game was over, and the Parkins family prepared to leave for the beach. Mrs. Wentworth passed them, stopped, and turned her horse back, to speak to them. "Hello. Enjoying yourselves?"

"Immensely," Hazel said.

"The Rover is running like a dream," she said to Paul. "You have the magic touch."

"I'm glad it's all right. It's a beautiful car."

She nodded. "When it runs. I have no use for things that don't work. Are you off?"

"Yes," Paul said, "we're going to the beach for a picnic."

"Where?"

"Crane's. If I can find it."

"Oh, don't go to Crane's. It will be a mob scene on Labor Day. And that awful parking fee." She pulled a thin wallet from her pocket and took out a card. "Go to West Beach. Use my cabana." She bent down and gave Paul the card.

"How kind," he said. "Thank you so much."

"Not at all. Anne and Hollister never use it, and I seldom get over there anymore. Tell Martin I said to treat you well. You know the way?" Quickly she gave Paul the directions.

"You are nice," Hazel said.

"Have fun." Mrs. Wentworth nodded and turned her horse.

Priscilla was dazed with joy. Using Hollister Wentworth's cabana was almost like meeting him. What if he did happen to come while they were there? She would faint.

"That was kind of her," Paul said to Hazel.

"She's Aries. Hates to waste a good thing, you know. Yes, she is nice. We'll have a lovely day."

Priscilla was pleased that Mrs. Wentworth liked her parents. She had a moment of panic when the gate guard looked at the membership card Mrs. Wentworth had given them, and then glanced at the pickup, but he waved them in with no change of expression. The man named Martin pointed out Mrs. Wentworth's cabana with professional courtesy.

About thirty people were at the beach, sunning, swimming, playing with a beachball. No one paid any attention to the Parkinses, and no Parkins except Priscilla wished anyone would. Peter had been missing the sea. He raced into the gray water and swam out so far that Paul went after him. They came back together, matching stroke for stroke.

The coldness of the water drove Priscilla out after a few minutes of cautious splashing. She helped Hazel put out the picnic lunch: cold chicken from the Puddleford flock, deviled eggs also from Puddleford hens, potato salad, carrot sticks, salted sesame seeds, buttermilk. Although Paul had been looking for a secondhand coal stove, Hazel still cooked with the Safari grill and a crane in the fireplace.

When Paul came in, he got a bottle of chilled wine from Martin to celebrate Labor Day. He toasted the castle. Hazel toasted Mrs. Wentworth. Priscilla toasted America. Peter fell asleep on the warm sand.

All afternoon they slept and swam and talked lazily and slept again. It was a relief not to be pounding nails and slapping on paint. Late in the afternoon when the sun began to go down, and almost everyone was gone, Peter said to Priscilla, "Race you to the rocky point," and he was off like a flash. He beat her, as he always had all their lives, but she no longer minded. He leaned on a high jagged rock, the wind blowing his hair around his face, his eyes shining. He said, " 'And oh, the sound of the seagulls! Have you heard it? Can you remember?' " He was quoting from one of the Narnia books that they had both loved so much and read so often when they were younger. Over their heads a half-dozen gulls wheeled and whistled and soared with the wind. She was glad he had thought of Narnia. He was really a very nice brother.

E L E V E N

J OURNAL: Labor Day—The most beautiful day! Polo in A.M. I fell slightly in love with Hollister Wentworth. He and his horse are Melody in Motion. Mrs. W. gave us her card for her beach club. Gorgeous day. Water too cold. Food wonderful. Peter quoted from a Narnia book. Then TWO THINGS HAPPENED. One slightly bad, one good beyond compare! ! ! Here's the slightly bad thing: when we walked out to the parking lot at the beach, two teenage boys and a girl were fooling around in front of us. One boy was drinking some kind of beer that I'm not familiar with, in an aluminum can. They all looked at the pickup when they went by it. One boy said something; they all laughed. I was getting mad and mortified. The boy finished his beer, lifted the can up as if it were repulsive, and dropped it in the back of the pickup. It made a loud rattle. The other two screamed with laughter. I was FULL OF RAGE. I would have run after him, but Hazel grabbed my arm. What Paul did was, he caught up with them without seeming to hurry at all. He took the can out of the truck and said to the boy, very calmly, "I believe you dropped your can." The boy looked scared. The other two snickered, and then they walked away as if they didn't know the boy. What treachery! The boy looked at the can as if he didn't know how to get away. "I'm sure you want it," Paul said. "It's recyclable." Which was really a brilliant stroke of irony, because you could tell this boy had never in his whole life cared whether anything was recyclable or not. But he couldn't look Paul in the eye. He took the can and muttered something unintelligible and walked off very fast after the two, who were already sitting in a blue Vega with the engine running. He got in and they sped off. I was in a purple fury, but the rest of the family seemed quite indifferent.

"Bad manners," Hazel murmured. How could she murmur? Even Peter wasn't interested.

"He humiliated us, that oaf did," I said. And Paul said, "Prissy, no one can humiliate you except yourself." I haven't had time to think about that yet, because a very few minutes later, the thing that is GOOD BEYOND COMPARE happened.

About five miles up the coast we had to stop at a little place so Paul could put some water in the radiator. The pickup leaks. This little place was just a pullover spot where you could see a good view of the ocean. I got out and sat on the stone wall. On the other side of the wall was a lot of kind of prickly bushes, the kind you see near the ocean, and some more big rocks, and a steep slope down to the sea. So I was sitting there looking at the view and I heard an odd sound. Kind of a scrambling sound, and some loose gravel shot past my hand. And then: THEN! there were these two paws on the wall near me and this gorgeous silky golden head and these two very dark fantastically beautiful eyes looking right at me. And I nearly fainted, he was so beautiful. It was an Afghan hound! ! ! He let me reach out and pat him, and he just kept looking at me. Then Peter saw him and came over. "It's an Afghan," he said. I knew that already, but I just said, "Shh, don't scare him." Peter said he didn't look too scarable. But there was something wrong. We coaxed him up closer. He was terribly thin, even for an Afghan, and his beautiful coat was matted and dirty. If you don't brush an Afghan all the time, he gets to looking like a rag bag. He didn't have any collar or tags or any identification. "He looks half-starved," Hazel said. "Here, dear." She helped him over the wall. Paul knelt beside him and looked him over and said he must have been gone quite a while from wherever he lived. I said how could anybody abandon a dog like that, an Afghan! And Peter said, "Oh, Pris, you're such a snob. You only like dogs in the upper income bracket." I denied it hotly but there is something in it; not in the money part, I don't care what they cost, but I do like purebred animals, because they are usually so handsome. It's no snobbier than Peter's preferring an MG to the pickup. So Hazel said, "We can't just leave him." And I said, of course not, we must take him home and I would care for him night and day. Paul said all right but no getting attached to him; he's a valuable dog and we'll have to find the owner. I thought to myself, we will cross that bridge when we arrive at it. So we took him home.

Hazel gave me her old hairbrush, and I fed the dog (he ate like a starving thing, which no doubt he was) and brushed him all evening. He is so beautiful, with his silky golden coat, it could break your heart. When he moves, his long hair ripples. He has that beautiful narrow long head, with a black muzzle, and his eyes are liquid and almost black and big. He is very dignified. I always wanted a borzoi, but this is better. I have named him Prince Hassan. Peter calls him Sheik, and Paul calls him My Liege. But the only name he answers to is Hazel's; she calls him Doggie.

T W E L V E

O N the day after Labor Day, Priscilla had to leave her dog for all day, which seemed very hard. But it was the last chance to register before school started.

"I'll guard him with my life," Hazel promised.

"It's supposed to be the other way around," Peter said.

Priscilla hugged Prince Hassan and said good-bye to him until Paul finally blew the horn on the pickup and she had to go.

Peter had one of his occasional morning jobs at the garage, washing cars for Pud, and in the afternoon he would work at the drugstore. Priscilla had a couple of hours to kill until he could go to the school with her.

She went into the Paper Store and ordered toast and milk and bought a morning paper. She read the headlines, the comics and her horoscope, although she didn't really believe in horoscopes, and she worked the cryptogram. Myrt was a little nicer than she had been the other time.

"How's your mother?" she said.

"Fine, thank you."

Myrt leaned her elbows on the counter and studied Priscilla. It made Priscilla nervous. "She's really different, isn't she," Myrt said.

Priscilla stiffened. "What do you mean?"

"Well, you know, different. So's Paul, if it comes to that. And old Pete." She laughed.

Priscilla felt her face getting hot. Who was this woman to criticize her family? Paul and old Pete indeed! She tried to think of something crushing to say.

"You ain't though," Myrt said. "You look like any little old Yankee kid."

Slightly mollified, Priscilla said, "Well, everybody's different."

"That's the truth." She pointed out the window at a bent small woman who was shuffling past the store. She was wrapped in a man's overcoat much too big for her. "Take old Angie, for instance. Her folks lived around here since my granddaddy's time. Look at the poor thing."

"What's wrong with her?"

"Paregoric addict."

Priscilla laughed, although she hadn't meant to; it was just so unexpected. "Paregoric?"

"Right. Been on it for years, got the habit before you had to have a prescription. Doctor can't figure where she gets it now, but she gets it, poor soul."

A man in work clothes came in, shoved his hat on the back of his head, and began a conversation with Myrt about a new bingo parlor. Priscilla thought of the ads in the Helsinki paper for Judo-Bingo. She and

Peter had laughed, trying to figure out possible ways of combining judo and bingo.

She paid Myrt and went down the street to the newspaper office. She had written out an ad for the Found Dog column, using Paul's phone number at the garage. As she gave it to the girl in the office, she crossed her fingers. She wished she knew how to put a spell on the ad so it would be invisible to the naked eye.

There was nothing left to do now but take a long walk through the residential part of town, looking with envy at the pleasant houses with their gardens, their dogs and cats and children and two-car garages. Someday she would live in a house like that. But meanwhile the castle and Prince Hassan were a big step in the right direction, if only she could keep them until they could go to Surrey, and perhaps, with fantastic luck, keep Prince Hassan forever. She had never been able to have a pet for very long, and finally not at all, because it was so difficult when you traveled a lot. The last pet she had had, and it still brought tears to her eyes to remember him, had been a big black cat in England. His name was Malcolm, and she'd left him with a schoolteacher named Miss Bates, because Malcolm refused to ride in any form of wheeled vehicle. She'd cried so hard, Paul had said, "No more." Of couse with Prince Hassan, he didn't think of it as Priscilla's dog. It was just a starving animal they'd rescued.

She sighed and wished the day were over so she could go home to Prince Hassan, while he lasted. She went to the library when it opened, and read the section on Afghans in the AKC Dog Book. Then she re-read a childhood favorite, *Bob, Son of Battle*, and cried a little.

She almost forgot about meeting Peter. She had to hurry to the school. He was waiting for her, sitting on an iron railing and swinging his long legs.

"You're late."

When she said she'd been absorbed in *Bob, Son of Battle*, he laughed. "When are you going to grow up?" He bounded up the steps, and she could tell he didn't in the least mind having to go into a new school. She followed him, with her heart pounding.

They had to stand in line behind four other students. The girl in front of Priscilla turned and looked at her. Priscilla gave her a tentative smile, and the girl said ;"Hi", but turned away again and talked to the boy in front of her. Behind the desk a young woman helped the students fill out forms, and an older woman banged away on a typewriter. Peter teetered back and forth on the heels and toes of his sneakers and whistled softly between his teeth. A boy in the line turned around and said, "Hi, Pete." Wherever they went, Peter always knew people. A group of girls came in, giggling and chattering. They picked up some schedules, exchanged remarks with the students in line, and went out again in a flurry of noise and motion. Everybody knew everybody. Priscilla wondered if she would ever get to knew them, let alone be accepted by them. She had gone so many years unsettled, unattached. She would never find her place.

"Yes?"

Suddenly she was at the desk and the secretary was

looking at her. She looked tired, probably sick to death of students. Priscilla had a wild impulse to say, "Oh, nothing, thank you," and flee. But she said, "I'd like to register."

Peter poked his cheerful face over her shoulder. "Both of us. She's my sister."

The young woman smiled a weary little smile. People always smiled at Peter, even when they were tired. She pulled two forms out of a pile. To Priscilla she said, "Your name?"

"Priscilla Parkins."

"Perkins?"

"Parkins with an *a*," Peter said.

"All right. Address?"

Priscilla hesitated for a fraction of a second. "Willow Lane." She waited for the woman to say "There are no houses up there except Puddlefords'," but she wrote it down without comment.

"Phone?"

"We don't have one yet."

The young woman looked up. "How can we get in touch?"

Priscilla couldn't think of anything to say.

"428-1134," Peter said. "You can reach my father at that number."

Why hadn't she thought of that. Nothing flustered Peter.

"Age?"

That was easy. So was the answer to the names of her parents and where her father was employed. She began to feel easier.

"Where were you born, Priscilla?"

That was a question she had forgotten to prepare for. For a moment she floundered. "Well . . . it's kind of . . ." A woman who looked like a teacher had come into the area behind the counter and she was looking at Priscilla. Priscilla felt faint.

Peter leaned against the counter. "She was born in the Red Sea," he said, "about midway between the Sudan and Saudi Arabia."

The secretary was not amused. "Look," she said, "I haven't got time for jokes."

"It's no joke. At least not to my mother. My father was a deckhand on this boat, and we were taking a cruise, half price. I was two years old at the time—"

"Look . . ." began the secretary, frowning.

The older woman, the woman who looked like a teacher, said, "Wait, Sue, I think he means it." She looked amused and interested.

"Thank you. Yes, I do mean it. A bad storm came up, you see, and the captain was drunk, so my father was running the boat, you know. My mother was expecting Priscilla but not right then, obviously, but in addition to everything else—I mean the drunken captain, the storm, and all—there was this nefarious character with a knife. He broke into my mother's cabin. He did not have good intentions, madam, believe me. My mother screamed, like a sensible woman, and someone told my father things were not as they should be. He got another chap to take the tiller, and he rushed to my mother's cabin. By this time someone was sitting on the villain's head. He was soon disarmed and tossed in the brig. So all was well and my mother was unhurt, but she surprised everyone by having her second child that very night."

The teacher laughed. "And where were you all this time?"

"I wish I could say I remember. They say I slept through it all."

The secretary, still skeptical, said to Priscilla, "Is he making it up?"

Priscilla wished she were a thousand miles away. "No. It's true."

"Are your parents U.S. citizens?"

"Yes," Peter said. "I was born in Iowa."

The teacher, looking at Peter, said, "What year are you?"

"I think it will amount to twelfth. My sister tenth. Most of the time our mother has taught us, courtesy of the American Overseas Correspondence School."

"I'm Miss Winston," the woman said. "You will have to take placement tests—make a note of it, Sue—but I tell you frankly, young man, I can hardly wait for you to arrive at twelfth-grade English."

"Thank you, madam." Peter made the quick little bow from the waist that he'd seen European boys make. "I, too look forward to it."

When they finally escaped from the school, Priscilla said, "Did you have to tell that crazy story about how I was born?"

"It was all true."

"But you make us sound like such nuts. They'll never accept us as ordinary Americans."

"Well, we aren't. Oh, come on, Sis, relax." He took

her by the elbow. "It was just one of those kooky situations."

"That we abound in. We'll be a laughingstock."

"Not if we laugh first."

"Tell Paul not to wait for me. I'm going to walk home."

"It's a longish walk."

"If there's one thing I've learned to do in my *fascinating* life, it's to walk." Before she had gone far, she turned to tell him she hadn't meant to be mean. But Peter was already out of earshot. She hoped he wouldn't think she was stuffy and bad-tempered. It wasn't that she wanted to deny the European part of her life. It was just that she longed to settle now into a groove where she could label herself: Priscilla Parkins, American teenager, descendant of Americans. A person needed to find out who she was and cleave to that identity. It would be something solid to lean up against. In Europe she was the odd one because she was an American. She hoped now that she wasn't going to be the odd one here, too. She ran the last quarter mile home, impatient to see her dog.

THIRTEEN

S CHOOL was, as Peter said, a mixed bag. He disliked the routine and the discipline of having to be certain places at certain times, but he enjoyed making friends. With Priscilla it was the other way around. The routine, which she had had so little of in her life, seemed solid and comforting, but the students frightened her.

At first it seemed all right. An attractive girl named Stephanie took her around and introduced her to teachers and students. But after a couple of days, just when she had begun to think of Stephanie as a friend, she stopped paying attention to Priscilla. Priscilla was crushed: Stephanie was obviously one of the most popular girls in school, and Priscilla had thought she was extremely lucky to be her friend.

"Don't take it personally," Peter said. "She was assigned to show you around. You can't expect to make instant friends the very first day."

But Peter himself made instant friends. He always had a little group around him, laughing at his stories and his comments. After Stephanie had turned away with a brief "hi" when Priscilla went up to her, Priscilla moved warily, talking to people only when they made the first move.

The friendliest person was Kath Puddleford, who was a senior and an honor-roll student. Everyone said she was brilliant in Latin and French, but sometimes Priscilla heard other girls making fun of Kath, her flat nasal voice, her broad blunt-featured face, and the flat-footed way she walked. She was easy to make fun of, but Priscilla liked her. They rode the school bus together and once in a while Mr. Puddleford brought them home.

Kath was not much of a talker. Often they walked in silence from the Willow Lane turnoff where the bus left them. She seldom asked questions, and she never mentioned the castle. Although Priscilla had been in Kath's house several times, she had not asked Kath to the castle. One afternoon, Hazel came across the meadow to meet them, Prince Hassan racing in circles around her and then hurling himself at Priscilla, his golden coat streaming out like banners. When Kath saw him, she was transformed. She stared at him with a radiance that Priscilla had never seen on her usually placid face.

"That beautiful dog!" she said. She watched him put his paws on Priscilla's waist, thrusting his panting face up at her like a scatterbrained puppy. "Oh, Mrs. Parkins, he is so beautiful!"

Hazel smiled at Kath, whom she liked. "Yes, isn't he."

"My father said you had a dog but I had no idea . . ."

Kath bent over Hassan, gently stroking the top of his silky head. "Is he one of Sonny Detheridge's dogs?"

Priscilla felt a chill. "No. Who is that?"

"He raises Afghans." She touched Hassan's ear.

"You love dogs," Hazel said.

"Oh, yes. I'm going to raise them when I get through school. Maybe Shelties, though I'm not sure. I keep changing my mind. There are so many breeds I like."

"Aren't you going to college?" Priscilla said. But her mind was on somebody named Sonny Detheridge.

Kath shrugged. "Father says I am. I'd rather not."

"I thought all American girls went to college."

Hazel laughed. "Prissy has very definite ideas about what Americans do."

Kath smiled at Hazel in a way that she had never smiled at Priscilla. They understand each other, Priscilla thought, and she felt left out.

"Come see us, Kath," Hazel said, as she and Priscilla started across the meadow.

"Why did you have to say that?" Priscilla said crossly, when they were out of earshot. "Now she'll be hanging around all the time."

Hazel looked at her quickly. "I thought she was your friend."

"Well, she is, but I don't want to devote my whole life to her." She knew she sounded nasty, but Kath had scared her about this Detheridge.

Hazel said, "Did something go wrong at school?"

"No." Tears stung her eyes, and she ran ahead of her mother, down toward the river, Hassan loping after her. Everything had gone wrong. It had been a terrible day. First she had forgotten the combination of her locker, just as she'd known she would. A girl had seen her struggling with it and had stopped. For a moment Priscilla thought she was going to help her, but then the warning bell rang and she left. Priscilla lived in horror of being late to class, and now she was going to be late because she couldn't get her math book out of her stupid locker.

Miss Winston came along and said, "Go to the office and ask Sue to give you the combination."

Priscilla felt desperate. "I'll be late for math."

"I'll walk you to class." And after Priscilla had finally gotten the locker open, Miss Winston went with her to math and said, "Don't mark her late, Miss Crandall. She forgot her locker combination." There was a snicker that Miss Winston stopped with a glare. She meant to be kind, but she had made them laugh at Priscilla, and then she had rebuked them with her glare, which made Priscilla the outsider, the teacher's pet.

But that wasn't as bad as what happened in social studies. When they were going to show a movie or have a speaker, several social studies classes met together. Today there had been a movie about a person's rights if he was arrested. It hadn't lasted the whole hour, so Miss Peterson had asked for discussion. Or had demanded discussion.

Miss Peterson was a formidable young woman, tall and broad-shouldered, with suspicious eyes and a sarcastic tongue. Priscilla was terrified of her. Miss Peterson had already made several snide remarks about people who thought they were too intellectual to live in their own country.

Many students were afraid of her, but unfortunately Peter was not one of them. Sometimes it seemed to Priscilla that Peter was simply unaware of hostility.

He raised his hand, and when she gave him a curt nod, he said, "It can be very difficult if you're arrested in a language you're not too familiar with."

Everyone laughed, and he said, "No, seriously, language is a kind of civil right in itself."

Miss Peterson smiled her dangerous little smile. "Have you been arrested in a foreign country, Peter?"

"No," he said, "but my father was."

Priscilla's heart sank. How could he not know he was playing right into that awful woman's hands? You could tell by the gleam in her eye that she expected to hear it was on a drug charge.

"Tell us about it, Peter," she said. She looked at one of her few favorites, an obnoxious boy named Fleming, and all but winked.

Priscilla tried to signal Peter but he didn't look at her. She gave up and stared at the floor.

"It was in Finland," Peter said.

"I'm sure it was," Miss Peterson said. The class laughed. Peter was already known for his tales of Finland. Why couldn't he see that Miss Peterson had turned their laughter against him.

"It was up in Lapland," Peter said. "He was picking cloudberries."

She frowned. "Cloudberries?"

"Yes. Cloudberries are wonderful. But only Finns are allowed to pick them. So my father was arrested.

He didn't know the Finnish word for cloudberries, so he didn't know what he was arrested for. It got to be so complicated, we almost had to call the consulate in Helsinki, but then my mother found the word in the dictionary, and she explained we didn't know, so they let him off with a fine."

"Ignorance of the law is no excuse," said Fleming in his pompous adenoidal voice.

But the others looked puzzled. Priscilla realized they probably thought Peter was putting Miss Peterson on, and that was a dangerous thing to do. She was scowling.

"What are cloudberries?" Susie Patterson asked.

"They're these marvelous golden, juicy berries that they make things with, liqueur, jam and pastries."

"Why can't you pick them?" Gerry Anderson said.

"Because they're scarce and it's a very short season. They're a valuable crop."

They didn't know whether to believe him or not. They looked at Miss Peterson for a clue.

"You are wasting class time with a cock-and-bull story, Parkins," she said.

"It's really true," he said. "I just wanted to make the point that when you can't communicate, you—"

She interrupted him. "I have spent the summer in Denmark and Sweden. There are no such things as cloudberries. Your head, Parkins, is in the clouds. Or should I say it's full of clouds. Or cloudberries."

Now the class laughed, reassured as to what line to take. They were disbelieving Peter, laughing at seeing him squelched. He looked around the room, for once at a loss. He didn't understand their not believing him. He glanced at Priscilla.

She raised her hand.

Miss Peterson, smiling and happy again, nodded at her. "Another Parkins to be heard from."

"What Peter said is true," Priscilla said. She didn't want to say it, but he was her brother and truth was truth. "They do have cloudberries and it is a restricted crop. I mean restricted as to who picks . . ." She broke off. She wasn't saying it right, and they were grinning.

A boy named Jimmy Donaldson, who was sitting next to Priscilla, had not joined in the mirth. Now he said, "Why don't we ask Mr. Haines. He's just across the hall."

Mr. Haines was the science teacher. Jimmy Donaldson half rose from his seat. He was a serious boy, with dark curly hair and dark-rimmed glasses.

"Sit down, Donaldson," Miss Peterson ordered. "We don't need Mr. Haines. I was all over the countryside in Scandinavia. I never heard of cloudberries. Parkins is pulling our leg. Parkins has a weird sense of humor."

Jimmy Donaldson was looking out the open door. "There he is," he said. "There's Mr. Haines, if you want to ask him."

It was a challenge Miss Peterson couldn't turn down without losing face. She went to the door. "Mr. Haines," she said in a jocular voice, "may we waste your time for a moment?"

Mr. Haines, tall, young, pleasant, stuck his head in the door. "What's up?"

"Have you ever heard . . ." Miss Peterson paused,

mockery in her voice. "Have you, in your botanical adventures, ever heard of cloudberries? *Cloud*berries, that is."

Priscilla held her breath.

"Sure," Mr. Haines said. "They only grow in Finland, as far as I know. They say they make great liqueurs. Ask the Parkins kids . . ."

The bell rang. Everyone got up and rushed for the door with more commotion than usual. No one was going to risk laughing in Miss Peterson's face. Somebody put his arm around Peter and swept him away, triumphant. Jimmy Donaldson and Priscilla were the last to leave the room. She wanted to thank him, but she was too upset to say anything. He glanced at her with his serious dark eyes, and then went on out of the door.

When she was in the hall, Priscilla heard Mr. Haines say, "What was that all about?"

And Miss Peterson's cold voice saying, "Chalk one up for Parkins. I said there was no such thing as cloudberries."

"Oh, lord," Mr. Haines said. "Why didn't you clue me in?"

"I tried to."

Priscilla walked down the corridor thinking bitterly, there's nobody who cares about the truth. Not even a nice-looking, honest-looking science teacher like Mr. Haines. Faculty stick together.

Now she lay down in a tangle of ferns and said to Hassan, "You can't trust adults." He whined softly and thrust his cold nose into the collar of her jacket. "I can't really trust anybody but you." For an hour they stayed there, moving only when the sun moved. Then she got tired of feeling sorry for herself and raced Hassan up and down the meadow until she was out of breath and his tongue lolled out of his mouth.

That night she quarreled with Peter for the first time in ages. Her father spoke to her reproachfully, and her mother looked worried. Later when she went to her room, she saw Hazel sitting cross-legged on her bed, the lodestone casket in her lap, staring with the unseeing look that meant she was deep into meditation.

Priscilla thought, she's consulting the lodestone about what to do with me. Well, it's going to take more than an old stone to tell her what to do about me. I was a misfit in Europe, and I'm a stranger in my own country. She went to bed and cried, and she let Hassan stay on her bed all night, although he took up a lot of room.

FOURTEEN

F OR two weeks Priscilla hoped and prayed that someone, anyone, would ask her to the Harvest Dance. She thought Jimmy Donaldson might. After the day of the cloudberry discussion, he often waited for her in the hall and talked to her, and a few times he had taken her to Conway's for a Coke. Jimmy wasn't like the other boys. He didn't tease or do any of that mock-insult thing that a lot of American boys seemed to do. He just talked about all kinds of things, like a real friend. She felt at home with him. But he didn't ask her to the dance. When Peter finally asked her, she felt humiliated. The little wallflower that her brother had to take care of.

"Why do you want to go anyway?" Kath said. "I never go. For one thing, nobody asks me." She laughed cheerfully. "With big flat feet like mine, who wants to dance?"

Priscilla felt embarrassed, but Kath was stroking Hassan's ears, apparently quite unconcerned about her lack of attraction for boys.

"My father says," Kath went on, "there used to be a song about 'flat-foot floozy with a floy-floy' That's me. I don't know what a floy-floy is but I figure it's just as well not to ask."

It was different with Kath; she really didn't care. Priscilla cared. For years she had pictured herself whirling around an American dance floor with a handsome American boy. Or even one that wasn't so handsome. Well, it would be her brother, and that wasn't how she had imagined it.

On their way to the dance Peter stopped at the drugstore to get a new handkerchief for the pocket of his jacket. He looked very nice. Poor Peter—he could have had his choice of half a dozen girls, but he got stuck with his sister. It was good of him. It wasn't his fault if she was an outcast. Sometimes she had the scary thought that even in Surrey it might have been the same.

When Peter came out of the drugstore, three young people came with him. One of the young men glanced toward the pickup and Priscilla turned hot and cold. It was Hollister Wentworth. She was afraid Peter would bring them over to meet her, and she was not sure she would be able to control her voice. Hollister had on blue jeans and a bright red flannel shirt. He looked beautiful. She hardly noticed the other boy, but she noticed the girl for a second, a tall, pretty, dark-haired girl in leather shorts and a dark green boat-necked sweater. She looked pale.

They went to a station wagon. When Peter got into the pickup, he said, "That was the Wentworths. Hollister and Anne and some other guy."

"Oh." Priscilla swallowed.

"The guys are down from Harvard for the weekend."

"Where does the girl go to school?"

"Some boarding school. But she's sick, so she's home. They're nice people." He whistled all the way to the school gym, as if nothing earth-shaking had happened.

Priscilla walked into the gym with her head up, trying to pretend that going to a dance with your brother was the most swinging thing a girl could do. Peter spoke to lots of people, and she did too, calling out gaily to people she hardly knew. Let no one dare to feel sorry for her! She even stopped to speak to Jimmy Donaldson, who stood alone near the band-stand.

"Hi, Jimmy. Nice to see you." She said it as casually as if it had never crossed her mind that he might ask her to the dance.

He gave her an odd look and said, "Good evening."

Two older boys called to Peter. "Hey, Finn, tell us about the midnight sun."

She wanted to hit them, and she hated the people standing nearby who laughed. One of them was Stephanie Collins, although she had seen Stephanie flirting like mad with Peter only the day before.

Peter grinned and said, "Well, man, it's like this: it's either up there or it isn't." He took Priscilla's hand and pulled her along to the locker room, where there was a pile of coats. Under his breath he said, "Jack-asses."

Priscilla looked at him in surprise. "I thought you liked all that kidding around."

He was unwinding the long scarf he had worn. "It's

the price you pay, I guess. But I'm getting sick of it. If I'm going to be a clown, I'd like to get paid for it." Then seeing her astonished face, he said, "Don't mind me. I like a lot of those guys, I really do. But some of them, like those two . . ." He made a face.

"I'll never understand brothers," she said. He laughed. She had said that a lot when they were children.

"We're ingrown, Prissy," he said. "We've spent so much of our lives with each other instead of with other kids." He took her coat and hung it up. "I know you and you know me, but it takes some doing to know other people."

"But I don't even know you," she said. "I didn't know you minded."

"Oh, most of the time I don't. Only, you know, they talk about last year's big game and their summer at the lake and this and that . . . because that's what they know. I talk about Europe because that's all I know. Why is it so weird?"

"Maybe we shouldn't have come back." She felt bad. It was partly because of her that they had come; she had longed so to come. And now Peter was unhappy, and she hadn't even noticed.

He smiled at her. "Cheer up. I didn't mean to spoil the party. And most of the time I don't feel this way." The band started to play, so loud that he had to raise his voice. "Madam, will you dance?" He made his stiff little bow and offered her his arm.

Paul and Hazel loved to dance and they had taught Peter and Priscilla early. Often the four of them spent an evening dancing to the stereo, everything from the tango and the polka to the current popular dances. Priscilla and Peter danced well together and they enpoyed it, but Priscilla knew she couldn't expect Peter to dance much with her tonight. There were all those other girls with an eye on him.

As they came around the floor, she saw why Jimmy Donaldson could not have asked her to the dance. He played the piano in the band. He was good. He played as if nobody else were in the hall, concentrating totally on the keyboard, his curly hair falling over his forehead.

"Donaldson is good," Peter said in her ear, and she felt obscurely pleased.

Several boys asked her to dance, but her enjoyment was spoiled by her shyness. They tried to talk to her, but most of them finally gave up. She was disgusted with herself for not being able to chatter the way other girls did, but she had never had much chance for that kind of casual social conversation and she didn't know how to handle it. Everything she thought of to say sounded too stupid, or else by the time she got up enough nerve to say it, the moment had passed. She felt all tightened up, and her voice sounded strained and high. They would never like her. They would think she was stupid. If she could only say, in a natural way, "Bear with me. I'm not used to this." But she couldn't say anything so spontaneous.

Once when Peter was dancing with her, he held her off and said, "What is it, Pris?"

"Nothing. I'm fine."

"You aren't. Aren't you having a good time?"

"Of course. Marvelous." She was afraid she would cry if she had to say any more.

"Jackson told me you're a neat dancer."

She wanted to say, "And did he tell you what a dazzling conversationalist I am?" But she was determined not to spoil Peter's evening. She made herself smile at him. "Did you tell him we're the rage of Europe?"

"Of course."

That dance ended with a great flurry of drums, and the clarinet player announced intermission. People began to mill around, finding partners, heading for the refreshments.

"You go," Priscilla said. "Stephanie is giving you the eye."

"She's mad at me because I didn't bring her to the dance."

"She's waiting for you. Go on." She gave him a push and turned away. She could stay in the coat room till it was over.

Jimmy Donaldson caught up with her at the door. "Excuse me," he said, looking at her in his serious way. "Will you have intermission with me?"

Surprised, she said, "Me?"

"You." He took her arm and guided her to a relatively empty corner. "Don't go away."

In a few minutes he was back with two styrofoam cups of punch and a paper napkin filled with cookies. "Excuse the inelegance." He put the cookies in her lap. "And the punch is deadly, but it's wet and cold." He drank it all at once, put down the cup, and mopped his damp face with his handkerchief. "Now I may survive."

"Would you like my punch? You're an awfully good pianist." It was the longest speech she had made to anyone all evening, except of course Peter, but it was only Jimmy Donaldson; she didn't feel nervous with him.

"No, thanks, to the first; and thanks to the second. More than one cup of that stuff would curdle your blood. I could dump yours in the potted palm, if you like."

She laughed. "No, I'll do my duty."

He sat down beside her and stretched out his legs. He didn't say anything for a few minutes, but the silence didn't worry her.

"I was supposed to play at the Club tonight. Twice as much money. But I made this sacrifice for my alma mater." Jimmy paused and looked past her at the clusters of orange balloons that hung limp from the rafters. "Actually I came because of you."

"What?" She thought she had misunderstood him.

He didn't answer. She was sure she had misunderstood him. She was glad she hadn't said anything foolish. She noticed that his eyes were hazel. She could have sworn they were brown, but now she saw the flecks of green.

"You're a lucky duck," he said, "to have been all over the world."

"Well, not really all over the world. Just Europe, and mostly Scandinavia."

"Just Europe." He shook his head. "I'd like to get on a boat and sail all over." He'd said that before. Probably he would do it. He was the kind of person you expected to do what he said he'd do.

"I'll come with you," she said lightly. "You'll need a crew."

He didn't laugh. Instead he said, "That's the idea."

She was confused because he didn't pick it up as a joke. "What is the idea?"

"That we'll do it together. Go to all the exciting and beautiful places, some you can show me and some you won't have seen either."

She was disconcerted. This wasn't the way Jimmy Donaldson usually talked. Usually they talked about mean old Miss Peterson and the politics of the Europeans, which Jimmy was interested in although Priscilla couldn't tell him much; and they talked about the climate in Scandinavia, and the skiing, and why Finnish kids had to learn Swedish as well as their own language. None of their talk had ever been personal.

"That's a really wild idea," she said.

"I can foresee it happening."

She grabbed onto a new possibility for a joke. "Don't tell me you're psychic."

"Certainly."

"I can't bear it." Now her voice sounded the way it did with other boys, strained and self-conscious. "My mother is psychic, that's enough." He smiled and she said, "I'm a very rational person. I'm logic-minded."

"I know something about you that you don't know."

"What?"

"Underneath that logic you have a strong strain of mysticism."

"Oh, no, you're wrong."

"You're a believer."

"What do I believe in?"

He waved his hand. "That's of no consequence. Believers can believe in anything, from the glory that was Greece and the grandeur that was Rome to trolls and leprechauns, gods, witches, anything. It's the act of belief that matters."

"Well, I have to have things proved."

"Only up to a point. To change the subject, the place you're living in sounds marvelous."

She looked at him uneasily. "I didn't know people knew about it."

"In a town this size everybody knows everything. I hope you'll invite me to see it sometime."

"Yes. All right." It made her nervous to think people knew about the castle.

"I used to go swimming out there; there's a great swimming hole. Then I'd go sit by one of the fireplaces and imagine I was British royalty. Not Henry the Eighth, though. He sounds to me like a nasty man."

For a minute she wanted to tell him about the woodpecker, and thinking it was Anne Boleyn's ghost, but she stopped herself. He would think she was crazy. "Where do you live?"

"Well, down the main road. Do you know where the Wentworth place is?"

She swallowed. "Yes, I think so."

"We live next door."

"You do?"

"Why do you look surprised?"

She didn't know why she was surprised. "I don't know."

"I suppose you're in love with Hollister."

She felt the blood rush to her face. "Hollister Wentworth? I don't even know him."

"That's all right. Every girl east of the Hudson is in love with him; it's an act of nature, like the law of gravity."

"Well, I'm certainly not. I've only seen him twice in my life."

"Unfortunately that's enough."

"Why do you dislike him?"

He looked surprised. "Dislike Hollister? I like him very much. He's a great tennis player and a terrific horseman." He studied her. "As you probably know. Do you know Anne?"

"No. I've seen her. Tonight in fact."

"Was she out? She's supposed to be in bed. She has mono."

"What's that?"

"Mononucleosis. The great American teenage disease. Mono and syphilis. No, sorry, I didn't mean to be gross. Mono is called the kissing disease, but it isn't necessarily. I had it for months, and I hadn't kissed anybody for three years, not even my mother." He bit into a cookie and made a face. "Sawdust flavored with artificial lemon extract. The Wentworths are my cousins, by the way."

"Really?" She was surprised.

"I know it's a ridiculous idea. We're the poor relations. Aunt Anna married a fortune, and my mother married my father, whose patients often forget to pay him. What would you be doing now in Finland?"

His changes of subject bewildered her. He was not like himself tonight. "Well, a year ago we were in

Lahti. It would be getting very dark, getting into long weeks when the sun never gets much above the horizon." She shivered, remembering the cold darkness. "My mother would be at the convent school teaching English. My father would be at the Volvo garage. Peter and I used to study in the morning and then go over our lessons with my mother when she got home."

"Did you have a hundred boyfriends?"

She laughed. "No. I didn't know any boys who spoke English. And when all you can say in Finnish is 'Good morning, two cabbages, ice cream, ten eggs, thank you, and good-bye,' it makes kind of a funny conversation."

"I can see that. But conversation isn't always what a boy has in mind."

He made her uneasy. She wished he'd go back to politics. "I didn't have many friends. Only a few girls, my mother's students, who came to practice English on me."

"Were you lonely?"

Of course she had been lonely, but she didn't like to say so. It seemed somehow like a criticism of her family. "Peter and I had fun. We used to go skating and sledding a lot."

The other band members were gathering on the bandstand. One of them called him. He glanced at them and stood up.

"You look very pretty tonight."

She said, "Thank you," but she looked at him as if he were a stranger.

"If I didn't have to play, I'd have asked you to the dance."

She felt herself blush. "Oh."

"Would you have accepted?"

"Yes, I . . . yes."

"Some other night then." And he was gone, pushing through the crowd, sitting at the piano, bending over it in total concentration as he brought his hands down on the keys.

She felt unreal. Had Jimmy really said what she thought he said?

"There you are," Peter said. "I lost you. Want to dance?"

"I'll sit this one out." And as he started to sit down beside her, she said, "Alone. You go dance, Peter."

"Sure?" He knew she feared being a wallflower.

"Yes, really. I want to think."

"Righto. See you."

But she couldn't get her thoughts into any kind of order. She stared at the swirl of dancers without seeing them. No boy had ever said things like that to her before. Her family sometimes said she looked pretty, but no boy. And that it should be Jimmy Donaldson of all people. It had been a surprising conversation, and she didn't know what to make of it. She remembered that he was almost seventeen. Maybe you began to change when you got a little older. Although it didn't seem to her that Peter had changed much. Well, she would have to think about it all.

FIFTEEN

JOURNAL: October 18—At the Harvest Dance last night I had my first experience with an American line. I didn't know what it was until I got home and thought about it, but that's what it was, all right. I've read about it in American magazines. A line is when a boy tells a girl a lot of sweet nothings that of course he doesn't mean, and of course she knows he doesn't mean it, and it's just a game. It's something like the Court of Love, in the days of Eleanor of Aquitaine, kind of a meaningless ritual that's pretty and everyone enjoys it without getting her feelings hurt. Jimmy Donaldson was the one with the line, and he really had me puzzled at first, because I had forgotten about lines and I thought he meant it. It's a good thing he didn't know I thought he meant it; he would have had a good laugh. I asked Peter if he used a line, and he said what did I mean. For once I know about something Peter doesn't know about. I didn't tell him, because then I'd have had to get into what Jimmy said and all. Jimmy Donaldson is Hollister Wentworth's first cousin. Lives next door. I think the best attitude I can take with Jimmy is one of being in on the joke, not annoyed or anything. Then he'll see I'm a regular American girl like anyone else. He might even tell Hollister that I'm really a good sport. It's very important in America for a girl to be a good sport.

SIXTEEN

PRISCILLA lay beside Hassan on the big wolfskin rug that someone had given Paul in Denmark. He had fixed someone's car, and they had given him the rug instead of money. Priscilla liked to lie on it, but she always felt bad about the wolves that had died to make it. Paul said not using it wouldn't bring them to life, but that wasn't the point.

Hassan had his paws across Priscilla, and every once in a while he stretched out his long head and gave her a slurpy kiss. Paul was fiddling with the new oil heater he had bought, which made the big room warm. Hazel was reading a booklet by Maharishi Mahesh Yogi, and now and then she read a sentence aloud, not to them but for herself.

"This room is hard to heat," Paul said, "because of the high ceiling."

"But cathedral ceilings are so nice," Hazel said.

Paul looked up. "You couldn't buy a beam like that today at any price. They don't cut wood in that size anymore. If you wanted a beam that size, you'd have to have it laminated."

" 'Knowledge is structured in consciousness,' " Hazel read. " 'Action is structured in knowledge; achievement is structured in action, and fulfillment is structured in achievement.' "

"Unless of course you could cut your own tree," Paul said, still looking up at the beam. "I wonder how much of the spiritual impact of a Gothic cathedral comes from the reminder of great trees."

Peter came into the room carrying some paper. "Here's how my English theme starts. Listen for a sec, Titania. The title is—in quotes so she won't say I plagiarized it—the title is: 'When Worlds Collide.' Here's how it starts: 'The summer that my father got into transactional analysis and my mother discovered transcendental meditation, the earth shook.' "

Hazel and Paul laughed. "That *was* a summer," Paul said.

Priscilla covered her ears with her arms. She didn't want to hear the rest of it. Peter was at it again, making the family a laughingstock. Why didn't they mind? It occurred to her that he never included her in his stories, except in a casual reference.

When he finished reading, she said, "How come you never put me in your stories?"

"You wouldn't think it was funny."

"No, I wouldn't. I don't think any of it is funny."

He shrugged. "I'm sorry." He looked hurt.

Hazel said, "It's very hard for a girl who's fifteen to laugh at herself. That's a kind of objectivity that comes later."

"If at all," Paul said.

"I suppose I have no sense of humor," she said.

"Yes, you have, Pris," Peter said. "You're just going through a period of adjustment. We all are."

She hated phrases like "period of adjustment." She didn't think of herself at all as a check mark on a psychological graph. She was Priscilla Parkins, of the Surrey Parkinses, part of a long, continuing chain but nevertheless herself and unique. She excused herself on the grounds of homework to be done, and she and Hassan went to her room.

She had gotten back an English theme that day herself, and it had depressed and discouraged her. She was not doing well at all in English, and she couldn't understand it. This theme, which got a C, had been a description of the house in Surrey. To her, it had seemed vivid, even poetic, and full of feeling. But the teacher had marked it all up with comments like "cliché!" "vague," "stereotype," and at the bottom she had written, "This is not a real house at all. You have put together all the 'quaint' little old houses you see around New England and you've plastered it over with gobs of sentimentality and cliché. You must write about real things, things you know."

But she had written about what she knew. Because Jimmy was there after class, she showed the theme to him. She had to complain to someone. Since the dance he treated her as matter-of-factly as he had before, so she had not had to worry about keeping up her end of the "line."

He read the paper carefully. "Well," he said. "I think—"

"You agree with her." She was ready to be furious with him. "But you're wrong. It's a very real house with real faded, weatherbeaten clapboards, real central chimney, real hollyhocks. It's my grandfather's house in Maine and I love it."

"What she means is, all houses of that type look like that. She doesn't see what you see—"

"I suppose if I'd put in about the wall caving in when Hazel hung up the washing in the dining room, that would have been a riot and I'd have gotten an A."

He looked for a moment as if he wanted to laugh, but he didn't. "It's hard to write about something you feel deeply about. I can't write about music for instance. What you've got here is kind of an abstraction rather than a real house, and your abstract house has abstract feelings inside it, nostalgia with a capital N, family feeling with capital F's, and so on. It's a while since you've seen the house, so it's all blurry with memory and love. When you see it again, you'll see a particular house, *that* house, with maybe a brick fallen out of the chimney, and paint worn thin near the door handle, and inside it there'll be a particular girl, you, Priscilla Parkins, with very specific feelings, and all the abstractions will become real and *you*. Do you see?"

She said she did, but she really didn't. An abstraction she had never understood. "Anyway," she said to Hassan, "you're a real dog." She sat cross-legged on the bed and closed her eyes. Sometimes she did this to see if she could meditate the way Hazel did, to see if there was anything to it. You were supposed to have a secret word, a mantra, that would lead your mind into blankness. She had tried different words, but they always had associations that distracted her; "dog" of course led at once to an awareness of Hassan; "wall" brought up an image of the stone wall by the castle that was brilliant now with flaming sumac. Tonight she tried "it." She closed her eyes very tight and concentrated on "it." But in a minute she was thinking "It is . . ." and then "It is eight o'clock," and then she smelled popcorn cooking, and she thought, "It is eight o'clock and I am hungry." It was no use.

"Come on," she said to Hassan, "let's get some popcorn."

To her mother she said, "Can I go get Kath?"

"Of course."

She and Hassan raced across the field. The grass was touched with frost, and there was a big orange moon low in the sky. It was the kind of night she had imagined when she thought of New England autumn. She felt much better.

Spot ran out to challenge Hassan as he always did, but nothing ever came of it. They circled each other, sniffed, and growled awhile, and then Spot slunk off toward the barn.

Mr. Puddleford came to the door, a newspaper in his hand and his glasses shoved up onto his forehead. "Come in, come in, young lady. Kath, the Parkins girl is here."

Kath looked pleased when Priscilla asked her to come over. She never came unless she was specifically asked, and often Priscilla just didn't think of it. While she was getting her jacket, Mr. Puddleford brought out a jug of cider.

"Here, give this to your old man. I promised it to him. Made it myself."

Looking past him Priscilla could see Mrs. Puddleford hunched forward in front of the TV set, watching a game show. She thought of saying hello, but she knew Mrs. Puddleford hated to be interrupted in the midst of TV, so she didn't go in.

"Paul is popping corn," Priscilla said, as they walked back across the meadow.

"Oh, good. Maybe I can gain another pound." Kath laughed and patted her plump stomach. Just before they got to the castle, they heard a car come along Willow Lane slowly. Kath grabbed Hassan's collar as he turned toward the sound.

"What is it?" Priscilla said. There were seldom any cars on Willow Lane. It was just a loop of dirt road connecting at both ends with the back road to the north.

"Oh, nothing. I just get jumpy."

"What about?"

Kath looked at her. "I saw Sonny Detheridge's station wagon downtown today."

"Who's he?" Priscilla said, but she knew.

Kath didn't answer for a minute. "I saw the ad you ran in the paper about finding Hassan." She looked up at Priscilla. "I prayed Sonny Detheridge wouldn't see it. Then I found out he was out on the West Coast for the dog shows."

"And now he's back?"

"I'm not sure. I just saw his wagon."

"You think Hassan is his?"

"I don't know. I think it's possible."

The sound of the car was gone now. Kath let go of Hassan's collar, and he raced toward the house. The stand of birches and pines between the castle and the road looked quiet and peaceful, as if no one ever came near them.

"Do you think I should tell this Detheridge about Hassan?"

"No. I do not. He doesn't care about his dogs except for the money. Anyway, Hassan may not be his. Don't mind me. I'm a natural-born worrier."

When they got to the house, Peter looked up from the popcorn shaker that he held over the fire. "Kath, you get to pour the melted butter because you've got a level head. Pris always dribbles it."

Kath laughed. "Okay, Peter, but I'm the type that drowns the popcorn." She hunched down beside him in front of the fire.

Priscilla strained her ears, thinking she heard a car again, but it was only the wind in the trees. She sat down with her arm tight around Hassan.

SEVENTEEN

P RISCILLA lay on her stomach on the unfinished section of stone wall in front of the castle, her sweater doubled under her to make her more comfortable. It was a Saturday morning, a warm Indian summer day. Paul and Peter were working a half day. In the back of the castle Hazel was beating a rug, and Hassan was with her. He loved to leap up and bite the corners of the rug as it swung on the line.

Priscilla closed her eyes and remembered vividly a day like this when they were in Rovaniemi, the little city in Lapland, on the edge of the Arctic Circle. It was September then, before they moved to Lahti. She had lain on the grass by the wide, slowly moving river that swept past the town, and she had half listened to the dull rhythmic thud of women beating their rugs with bamboo beaters. It was a familiar Finnish sound. Across the river the gently sloping fells had been dark green and gold, quieter than New England's flaming fall colors, but very pretty. She wondered if she could

write a theme about that without being called senti-
mental and abstract.

She lifted her head as something moved out in the
meadow. It was a man on a horse. She sat up. There
was another horse with a girl on it a little way behind
him. As they came closer, she saw that the girl was
Anne Wentworth, and the man one she had seen at
the polo game. He was a middle-aged man in tweed
riding pants, black boots, a short-sleeved shirt, and, at
a jaunty angle, a narrow-brimmed tweed hat. Priscilla
remembered from somewhere, probably England, that
those tweeds for informal riding were called rat-
catchers.

"Mornin'." The man touched a finger to the brim
of the hat.

"Good morning." She swung her legs down and
stood up.

Anne Wentworth came up at a slow trot. She
nodded to Priscilla, looking pale.

"I'm checkin' out the course for the hunt," the man
said. "I'm Con Kelleher."

"How do you do," Priscilla said. "I'm Priscilla
Parkins."

"I know. We usually cut across this place here when
we hunt out this way. You folks won't mind?"

"No, of course not. It's not our land anyway."

"That's right, it isn't." But he smiled in a friendly
way. "I'll be coming by real early in the morning with
the drag."

"You don't hunt a real fox, do you?"

"No. That's why I lay out a drag course."

"Con uses a bag with anise in it," Anne said. "The hounds follow the scent."

He was looking past Priscilla at the castle. "I see you folks did a mite of fixing up."

Priscilla looked at him sharply to see if he was making fun or being critical, but his face was expressionless. "We rent it from Mrs. Jonathan Wilder."

The man looked at Anne. "That what Sally goes by nowadays?"

Anne smiled. "That's the latest." She leaned forward suddenly and put her hand to her face. "I feel sick, Con."

Instantly he swung his leg over his horse and went to her. "I told you. You're supposed to be in bed."

"Don't scold me now." She let him help her out of the saddle. "Just let me lie down a few minutes. It'll go away."

"You come inside." He glanced at Priscilla. "You folks won't mind."

"Of course we don't mind." Priscilla didn't know whether to take Anne's other arm or not. Instead she took the horse's reins and hitched him to a stone post.

Hazel came around the house and stopped.

"It's Anne Wentworth," Priscilla said. "She's sick."

"I'm sorry," Anne said faintly.

"Oh, bring her in," Hazel said. "We'll take care of her." She took Anne's arm. "Poor child. We'll fix her up. Pris, go take the spread off your bed."

The man shot her a look of approval. "I'll give her mother a jingle. You folks got a phone?"

"No," Hazel said, "but my husband will be home soon. He'll see that she's taken care of."

"I'll take her horse along then." He looked quickly and appraisingly around the living room. "You lay down now, Anne, till you're all right. I'll call your mother as soon as I get back to the Club." He nodded to Hazel. "Thank you, madam."

Priscilla pulled down the bedspread, glad that she had changed the sheets that morning. Hazel dried her sheets outdoors, and they always smelled so good. Anne lay down and closed her eyes.

"I'm really sorry," she murmured.

"I'm sorry you're sick, but I'm glad you're here," Priscilla said. She wanted to add "If you'd only brought your brother."

Anne spoke in a languid voice, not opening her eyes. "Uncle James told me to stay in bed in the mornings, but it's such a bore. You think you feel okay, and then all at once you feel like the straw man in *The Wizard of Oz*."

Hazel came in and spread the blanket gently over her. "You just take it easy, dear," she said. "I'll make you a cup of sassafras tea."

Anne opened one eye. "Sassafras tea?"

"It's better than it sounds," Priscilla said. She noticed when Anne's hair fell back from her face that she had a thin white scar from the corner of her eye almost to her mouth. She wondered what had happened.

When Hazel brought the tea, Anne was already asleep, so Priscilla drank it, in the living room with her mother.

"Mono?" Hazel said, when Priscilla explained about Anne. "I hope she's taking plenty of vitamins."

"Dr. Donaldson is her uncle."

"Oh, she's sure to be all right then." Hazel had met Dr. Donaldson in the drugstore. Her instant judgments sometimes irked Priscilla, but with this one she agreed. Dr. Donaldson was Jimmy's father and Hollister's uncle, after all.

Hazel had gone back outside when Anne came out of the bedroom some time later.

"Do you feel better?" Priscilla said.

"Yes, thanks. Oh, what a beautiful Afghan." She held out her hand, and Hassan sniffed at it delicately. "Do you smell the dogs? What's his name?"

"Prince Hassan."

"Prince Hassan, you're gorgeous. He looks like one of Sonny Detheridge's dogs. Did you get him from Sonny?"

"No."

"Do you show him?"

"No."

"I show Mother's corgis sometimes. It's fun. You ought to show him." She knelt and put her hands on his legs. "I'm no authority on Afghans, but he looks awfully good to me. What kennel did you get him from?"

Priscilla swallowed. Several stories raced through her mind, but Anne was looking at her with clear gray eyes. "I found him."

Anne sat back on her heels. She looked distressed. "Oh. I see."

Now Priscilla wished she had lied. Anne would know who owned him, and it would be all over.

"You're afraid you'll have to give him up," Anne said. "Oh, that would be awful."

"I put an ad in the paper," Priscilla said. "My father asked around."

"Where did you find him?"

"The day we went to your mother's beach club. Near there."

"Oh." Anne looked concerned. She stroked Hassan's nose.

"He was starving," Priscilla said. "He looked awful. His coat was all matted and dirty."

"Oh well, then, someone must have deserted him."

But Priscilla knew Anne didn't really believe that any more than she did. "Or he ran away."

"Sonny's kennel is over that way, but Sonny isn't here. He's in California at dog shows. He's been gone a couple of months."

"Then it couldn't be his." Priscilla's spirits rose.

"Unless he didn't take them all. He leaves somebody at the kennel." She sat frowning, thinking. "Listen, even if it is his, if he was that careless, he doesn't deserve the dog. He's got scads of them anyway. It's not as if this dog were his pet. Did he have a tag?"

"No, not even a collar."

"Well, if I were you, I'd stop worrying. Just don't take him around town much." She got up. "And don't worry about me. I'd die before I'd tell."

Gratefully Priscilla said, "Thank you very much."

"I love your house."

"You do?" Priscilla couldn't believe it.

"Yes. It's so original. I love that hanging. Is it from Europe?"

"Yes."

"It's beautiful. You've had a fabulous life, haven't you."

Before Priscilla had recovered from the idea that Anne Wentworth thought the Parkins' life was fabulous, Mrs. Wentworth appeared in the doorway to take Anne home. Hazel came in to greet her, and Mrs. Wentworth, too, exclaimed over the charm of the house.

"You have so much imagination. Look, Anne, they've made chairs out of stumps and rocks." She sat down. "And they're comfortable."

Hazel smiled. "Lots of foam rubber."

Mrs. Wentworth patted Hassan, and Priscilla held her breath. But nothing was said about him.

"Would you like some tea?" Hazel said.

It went through Priscilla's mind for just a moment that Hazel might be lonesome here. In Europe she had made friends easily, but here she saw almost no one.

"It's sassafras tea," Anne said.

"Delicious." Mrs. Wentworth continued to look around with frank interest while Hazel brought the tea. "You liked living in Europe, did you?"

"Yes, very much," Hazel said. "Especially in Finland. Life is simpler, somehow." She handed Mrs. Wentworth her cup of tea. "My husband left the theological seminary because he felt he was getting caught up in something very complex that ought to be simple."

"Yes, I can see that. We do complicate everything. Did he find his answers in Scandinavia?"

Hazel smiled. "I think the only answer we both feel

sure of is that the answers are always just out of reach."

"But worth pursuing?"

"Oh, yes. One must pursue them."

"I love this tea. I suppose in a country like Finland there isn't so much to get in your way, throw you off your course, as there might be here?"

"Exactly." Hazel said it eagerly, as if she were happy to find someone who understood.

"Why did you come back? Or am I asking personal questions? Yes, of course I am. I have a bad habit. But my motives are pure." She smiled.

"Oh, it's nice to talk to someone who's interested." Hazel told her about the inheritance in Maine, and the need to see the property. "And we felt we owed it to Priscilla to let her have some time in the States. She misses it."

"You're crazy," Anne said. "I'd give anything to live the way you've lived."

Mrs. Wentworth laughed. "The grass is always greener."

"I think it's boring to go on living in the same place generation after generation," Anne said. "I'm going to live in San Francisco or Vancouver or somewhere exciting."

Priscilla was too amazed to reply. She had been envying Anne her beautiful home and the fact that Wentworths had lived there for almost three hundred years. People were certainly surprising.

Hazel was telling Mrs. Wentworth about the family they had spent the previous summer with in northern Lapland. As Priscilla listened, she felt suddenly homesick for Lapland, and for Sylvie and Kolli, and their other Lapp friends. It had been a wonderful summer, fishing and swimming every day, and getting to know all those active, alive people. She and Peter had loved it. She must remember to tell Jimmy about them.

"Pris saw a white reindeer," Hazel was saying. "That's very good luck." She smiled at Priscilla.

"Seeing any kind of reindeer sounds like good luck," Anne said. She looked at her mother. "Reindeer! Imagine!"

"We saw lots of them," Priscilla said.

"We must go to Finland some summer," Mrs. Wentworth said to Anne.

"Do let us know if you do," Hazel said. "We have such good friends. They would love to entertain you." Her face lit up as she said it.

"You miss them," Mrs. Wentworth said gently.

"Oh, yes," Hazel said. "Yes, I really do."

Mrs. Wentworth looked at her a moment. "Sally Weston must be glad you're here. She always fusses so about the taxes."

Hazel hesitated. Then she said, "We have never heard from her."

Priscilla was startled. Why was Hazel telling that? But she knew why. Like Anne, Mrs. Wentworth looked at you with those clear eyes, and you found yourself telling her the truth.

She looked puzzled. "I understood you had rented . . ."

"Well, in a way. I wrote her that we would like to rent it and that Paul would make part of it habitable. I sent her a check for the rent, and . . . we just moved in."

For a moment Mrs. Wentworth didn't answer. Then she laughed, a hearty, pleased laugh. "That's marvelous. Someone who can take on Sally. But you did take a risk, I suppose."

"Yes. It seemed worth it."

Mrs. Wentworth looked thoughtful. "Has Sally cashed your check?"

"No."

"When she does, you'll be safe, I should think. Keep on sending them right on time. Sally finds money hard to resist." She put down her teacup. "I must take this child home. She should be in bed." At the door she said, "If Sally gives you trouble, let me know. She's my third cousin, and you know how New England families are. We all have something on each other."

Anne laughed. "Mother."

"Well, you know, dear, I don't mean blackmail."

"She does though," Anne said to Hazel. "If she thinks it's a good cause, my mother is very skilled at blackmail."

"We'd better go before you destroy my reputation." Mrs. Wentworth opened the door. "Thank you for succoring my wayward child and for the lovely tea. Please come and see me."

Priscilla and Hazel walked with them to the car. Mrs. Wentworth looked back at the unfinished walls and towers. "Poor Tommy Weston. It's even sadder than a real ruin, isn't it. A dream never fulfilled."

"It was a crazy dream," Anne said.

"It might not be your dream, but it was his." She shook hands with Hazel. "But half a dream is better than no dream, isn't it."

Hazel smiled. "I think so."

Priscilla kept her hand on Hassan's collar as Mrs. Wentworth turned the car around in the field and headed back toward the road. She had never thought about Mr. Weston much before. It *was* sad. She leaned over and put her cheek against Hassan's silky head. And in her mind she prayed: "Don't let Mr. Detheridge come."

EIGHTEEN

PAUL woke Priscilla early, as she had asked him to, so they could watch the hunt. Peter decided he'd rather sleep, and Hazel stayed in the house. She didn't say anything, but Priscilla knew hunts upset her even when they didn't hunt a real fox. "It's a symbol of something cruel," she had said once. "It frightens me."

Kath came over and joined Paul and Priscilla on the low wall that led to the entrance of the castle. Hassan, to his dismay, was shut inside with Hazel so he wouldn't join the hounds, and although Priscilla didn't speak of it, so the hunters wouldn't see him and perhaps recognize him as a Detheridge dog.

When Paul went inside for a moment for a second cup of coffee, Priscilla said, "I told Anne Wentworth about how I found Hassan."

"Oh. You did?" Kath looked worried.

"She thought he was a Detheridge dog. She said she wouldn't tell."

"No, I don't believe she would." Kath frowned. "I

say if Sonny was stupid enough to let a dog almost die like that, he doesn't deserve him. He treats dogs like a commodity, like soybean futures or something."

"I suppose sooner or later I'll have to talk to him though."

"Don't do it." She swung her heels against the wall. "Unless you could buy him?"

"I don't have any money. And Paul can't afford an expensive dog."

Paul came back then. "Do you ride, Kath?"

"Yes, but I'm not good. I flop around like a sack of grain."

He smiled. "You're always so hard on yourself."

"I face facts." She cocked her head, listening. "Here they come."

The high baying of the hounds came to them on the light wind, growing louder very quickly.

"We'd better back up," Kath said. "We might get run over."

They moved back to the other side of the low wall, up near the arched entrance.

"Here they come." Paul pointed across the field.

The hounds swarmed into view, baying in high, excited voices, and right behind them came the hunters in their "pinks," riding hard across the field in a loosely formed wedge shape. Con Kelleher had set the trail up to the low wall opposite the one where Priscilla and the others stood, through the arched entrance, and off across the open courtyard, over the unfinished wall on the other side from the Parkins' living quarters, and through the grove of trees to the dirt road.

The din and the milling about of the dogs made

Priscilla shrink back. Paul put his arm around her. She had never seen a hunt up close like this before. It was colorful and exciting, but she also understood Hazel's aversion to it.

As the dogs swarmed over the wall, and the first horseman cleared it in an easy jump, Kath said in Priscilla's ear, "Mr. Wentworth. Master of the Hounds." The other riders came behind him so fast it was hard to distinguish one from another. She looked for Hollister Wentworth, but he wasn't there. Probably he was at Harvard, she thought.

A horse stumbled and shied at the wall, and a young woman was thrown. She rolled quickly out of the way of the horses behind her, who were coming too fast to stop. Paul started across to help her, and one of the horsemen turned back, but she caught her horse's bridle, remounted, and brought him over the wall. The horses followed the hounds through the entrance, and when the last one was through, Paul and Priscilla and Kath ran to the courtyard to see them clear the wall and disappear—red coats, black velvet caps, sweating horses—among the trees. There was a confusion of barking as the hounds lost the trail for a minute, at the road. Then they picked it up and scrambled into the woods on the other side.

Paul said, "Well, that's that. Come in and have some pancakes, Kath." And in the kitchen he said to Hazel, "It seems like an odd pastime for grownups, doesn't it."

"It's so pretty though," Priscilla said. "And exciting."

Hazel shook her head, but she didn't say anything. Peter came strolling into the room looking sleepy.

"How was it?" he said.

"Great," Priscilla said.

"They really make a racket, don't they."

Paul picked up the platter of pancakes and put it on the table. "I suppose it's a harmless way of letting off aggression."

"When you come right down to it," Kath said, "all sports are childish."

Paul smiled at her. "Kath the philosopher." And later when she had gone home, he said to Priscilla, "I like Kath."

On Monday, Priscilla couldn't wait to tell Kath that she had been invited to Stephanie's slumber party the next Friday. She had dreamed for years of going to a slumber party, although she had only read about them and had no clear idea of what they were.

As soon as she told Kath, she wished she hadn't. Kath had not been invited. Perhaps she would feel hurt.

But Kath just said, "Oh, when you've been to one slumber party, you've been to them all. The one thing you can be sure of is that you won't do any slumbering. It's a gab fest, that's what it is, with food."

"She only asked me because she has a crush on Peter."

"If you want to go, go. Don't worry about motives."

"But if you don't like them, maybe I won't like them."

"*Non disputandum est.*"

That evening when Paul came home, he tossed the mail to Hazel and said to Priscilla, "How was your day, princess?"

Priscilla was telling him about the slumber party when Hazel suddenly said, "We're saved!" She had the bank statement in her lap, and she was looking at a canceled check. "Sally Weston cashed our check."

"Beautiful!" Paul said. "We're not squatters anymore." He looked at the check. "I was getting nervous. People have been asking roundabout questions."

"Nervous!" Hazel said. "I've been worried out of my mind."

Priscilla looked at them. She hadn't dreamed they were worried.

"It's nice to be legitimate," Peter said.

"And you had the foresight to write 'rent' on the check," Paul said. "I'll even feel safe getting that wood range we've been looking at."

Peter made a low bow. "Hail to Titania. Hail to thee, blithe lodestone."

"Well, it wasn't the lodestone," Priscilla said. "It was money."

Hazel looked at her and shook her head, smiling. "Prissy, Prissy of little faith."

Priscilla thought of Jimmy Donaldson saying she was a believer. He was wrong.

Hazel slit open another envelope. "What's this?" She read it and looked up at Peter. "Is this your handiwork?"

"What's that?" he said innocently.

She read it aloud. "The student council of Naumkeag High School invites Mrs. Parkins to address the student assembly next Friday morning at ten, on the subject of transcendental meditation."

"Oh, no!" Priscilla said.

Peter shot her a look of annoyance.

"How did this come about?" Hazel said.

"They were intrigued with that theme I wrote about Paul's t.a. and your t.m. They asked me if you'd come."

"Hey, that's great," Paul said. He grinned. "I don't hear them inviting me, though. Don't they like t.a.?"

"Well, they've heard a lot about that; we had it some in psych. But they're really curious about transcendental meditation."

Priscilla said, "They just want something to laugh at."

The light went out of Hazel's face. "Well, I'll have to think about it." She got up and went outside to feed Hassan.

"I want to talk to you, Pris," Peter said. He looked angry. "Now." He went toward her bedroom.

She followed him. She was angry, too. He had no right to set up Hazel for a thing like that. "What is it?" she said shortly.

"I'll tell you what it is. I think you ought to cut out thinking you can run this whole family to your specifications."

She was shocked. He had never spoken to her like that. "What do you mean?"

"You know what I mean. You're always putting Hazel down—"

"I do not."

"Yes, you do. You frown at her clothes, you look

superior about the lodestone, all that. And you do the same to me. You sulk because I write a theme about my own parents. Just because you want to be a conventional little dope, like those other girls—which incidentally you'll never be. You want them to think we're the all-time typical American family, with two cars in the garage and a television in every room and a standing rib roast in the oven. Well, anybody with his head screwed on right can see that we're not, we never have been and we never wanted to be."

"I wanted to be." She turned her head away so he wouldn't see the tears.

"Okay. You can do what you want, but you can't expect the rest of us to fall into step just to back you up." He paused, and when he spoke again his voice was gentler. "Pris, I don't mean to yell at you, but Hazel would have fun speaking at that assembly. About all she ever gets to do is take care of us; she's got a good brain, I like to see her get a chance to show it. Don't spoil it for her."

"They'll make a fool of her. Even you talked about hating being a clown."

"Oh, that was once, and it's only a few kids that are that way. Do you think I'd let Hazel do it if I thought that could happen?"

"You don't know those kids."

"I know them a lot better than you do. You think Stephanie is so great. She's got a head full of cotton."

"You don't act as if you thought so."

"She's pretty, and she can dance. Period. But there are plenty of other kids, like Kath and Jimmy Donaldson and Peter Henderson and a lot of people who would really be interested in hearing Hazel. They're the ones that count." He put his hand on her shoulder. "Go tell her she ought to go, will you?"

She didn't answer, and in a moment he went away. She stood staring out the window, trying not to cry. It seemed to her that what he said was unjust. She felt Hassan's cold nose in her hand. All she wanted was a normal life and her own dog. It didn't seem like such a lot to ask.

But if it meant all that much to Peter, she would tell Hazel she might as well go. She just wouldn't go herself. She'd manage a sick headache or something. Only that was the day of the slumber party. Oh, what a mess Peter was always getting them into.

When Hazel came to call her to dinner, Priscilla said, "You better go to the assembly, Mother. It means a lot to Peter."

Hazel looked away. She straightened the spread on the bed. "I don't want to embarrass you, Priscilla. I guess Peter will survive."

"But you don't understand . . ." And suddenly Priscilla was crying.

Hazel sat down beside Priscilla on the bed. "Prissy, Prissy, there's nothing to cry about."

It was a long time since she had cried so hard. She had trouble getting her words out. "I didn't mean to hurt your feelings. I know just as well . . . just as well as Peter does, how smart you are. You're *too* good for ordinary people, that's the whole"—she caught her breath trying to stop crying—"the trouble."

Hazel laughed a sad little laugh and put her arm

around her. "I think we're kind of hard on you, dear. We're all so used to going our own way."

"I want you to come, really I do." And now she really did. "I'm just . . . I get so scared." She was crying again.

Hazel held her close. "I know. It's a scary world sometimes. But you're such a nice girl, Pris; just be yourself and people will love you. Don't worry so much. We'll try not to disgrace you."

"Oh, you don't." Priscilla sat up and mopped her face with a Kleenex. "I don't know what I want. I get what I think I want and then it scares me half to death. I'll probably be sick to my stomach all day before that darned slumber party."

"They just sit around and talk."

She nodded. "That's what Kath says. You will speak to the assembly, won't you?"

"If you want me to."

"Yes, I do."

"It would be interesting." She got up. "I'll bring you your dinner if you like."

"Oh, thank you. I would."

Later Peter brought her a dish of pudding. "This is baptismal pudding," he said, "the first thing Hazel's baked in the new range." He put it down and kissed Priscilla lightly on the cheek and went out again.

N I N E T E E N

JOURNAL: November 21—I wish I would hurry up and be sixteen. I don't think I can stand it much longer being fifteen. Hazel says it's a difficult age. I say it's pure hell. I don't know who I am or what I want or how to behave. I hurt my mother's feelings and make my brother mad and nobody at school likes me and I don't know what to do. Only my dog loves me. I can't stand myself.

TWENTY

THE day that Hazel was to give her talk to the school assembly was cold and rainy with a dense gray sky. Wet leaves were beaten down off the trees into sodden piles like old cornflakes that had been sitting in a bowl of milk too long. At least that was the image that went through Priscilla's mind as she turned up the collar of her parka and ran for the truck. Hazel was not coming to the school until later; Paul would come home to get her.

Priscilla huddled between Paul and Peter on the torn seat of the truck. Even Peter looked depressed. He had come to Priscilla the night before, worrying. "What if you're right?" he had said. "What if they think Titania is an oddball, a freak even?" He had looked so dejected, Priscilla had tried to cheer him up, although she felt far from cheerful herself. By the time she got through trying to convince Peter that Hazel would be a success, she had also cheered herself up for a little while, but it hadn't lasted. She wished she knew what Hazel was going to wear. That didn't seem important to Peter, but Priscilla knew how much it would count in the school's decision whether or not to accept her. Especially with the girls; that would be the first thing they'd notice. She crossed her fingers now in the truck, trying to will Hazel to wear something conservative, or at least conservative as she had. She hadn't mentioned it to her because she knew it would hurt Hazel's feelings, and she'd done enough of that.

Only Paul was in a happy mood. "Give your mother a great big hand," he said when he let them out. "I wish I could be there."

Priscilla went through the first two periods of the day in an increasing state of nervousness and absentmindedness. Even Miss Peterson's sarcastic remarks failed to reach her.

When she heard the bell ring for assembly, she began to feel sick to her stomach. For a minute that seemed almost providential; she could skip the assembly on the grounds of illness. But of course she couldn't really do that. It would be too disloyal. She was glad to find Kath beside her when she filed into the auditorium. Kath took her arm.

"How do you feel?"

"Scared out of my mind," Priscilla whispered.

Kath smiled. "Don't worry. She'll be terrific."

They sat down next to the aisle about halfway back in the auditorium. Jimmy Donaldson sat behind Priscilla. He leaned forward and tossed a newspaper clipping into her lap. She looked at it. It was a brief notice in the local paper that Mrs. Paul Parkins, who with her family had been residing in Europe for several years, was to speak at the school assembly on the subject of transcendental meditation. The members of the PTA and the school board had been invited to attend.

Priscilla showed it to Kath. "I didn't know they'd invited outsiders." She turned her head and saw half a dozen mothers sitting near the back of the hall.

"My father's coming," Kath said.

Priscilla was astonished. "Your father?"

"Well, he's on the school board, and you people are like his family, he said." Kath looked faintly apologetic. "I hope you don't mind."

"Of course not. I was just surprised."

The hall quieted down as the principal came out onto the stage and held up his hands. The bell rang. He gestured to the students to rise, and they all got to their feet with a great clatter and shuffle. He led them in the pledge of allegiance to the flag that stood at the side of the stage. They sat down again. He read the announcements for the day, but Priscilla didn't hear a word he said. What if Hazel hadn't gotten there? Sometimes she was vague about time. Priscilla couldn't decide whether it would be better or worse if she didn't show up. Her hands felt clammy. She tried to find Peter in the big auditorium, but she didn't see him. He was probably as scared as she was, maybe more so because it had been his idea. She swallowed and tried to ignore the nausea.

The president of the student council made some announcements, and then the head of the athletic club gave them a pep talk about the upcoming football game. Four cheerleaders whirled and twirled their way around the stage, batons flying through the air, and then they led the student body in a few yells. Obediently Priscilla raised her voice for South Naumkeag.

The principal returned to the front of the stage and waited for the noise to subside. He raised his hand impatiently to quiet the last ripples of sound. "This morning we are privileged to have a guest speaker of unusual interest. Such unusual interest, in fact, that we have invited our PTA and our board members to join us. I see that a number of them are present, and I take this opportunity to welcome them among us on this occasion."

Priscilla stared at her hands in her lap and thought desperately, "What are we doing in this country? We don't belong here."

The principal went on. "Our speaker, the mother of two of our students, has had a most interesting life." He consulted a tiny piece of paper that he held in the palm of his hand. "Born in Iowa, attended Columbia University in New York City . . ."

". . . and dropped out," Priscilla thought.

"After her marriage, she and her husband, and later her two children, traveled extensively in Europe. They have lived in England, in Norway"—he glanced at the notes again—"in Germany briefly, and for the past two years in Finland. Both our speaker and her husband are interested in philosophy and theology, and it is more or less in this field that our guest will address us today."

Kath groaned under her breath and said in Priscilla's ear, "If he leaves her any time."

"The subject, of much interest in our troubled times, is transcendental meditation. And I introduce

to you now our guest speaker, Mrs. Titania Parkins."
He swept his arm back toward the wings and half-
turned in an attitude of welcome. Nothing happened.

Priscilla wrung her hands together until they hurt.
There was the beginning of a wave of giggles in the
hall. The principal looked sharply at the students and
then took a step toward the wings. Then Hazel appeared. Even from halfway back in the auditorium,
Priscilla could sense the principal's relief. He reached
out for the microphone with one hand, as if he were
going to present it to her, and with the other hand he
waved her on.

Hazel came on with her quick, long-legged walk,
her head up, smiling at the students. But as she came
closer there was an odd sound, a kind of rhythmic
clumping. At first Priscilla couldn't make out what it
was. Then it came to her. Although Hazel had dressed
in her most conservative dark blue, full-skirted dress,
she was wearing her high-heeled wooden clogs, and as
she came closer to the speaker's stand, the mike picked
up the sound of the wooden shoes on the wooden
stage. Priscilla put her hand to her mouth in horror.
Now they would really laugh. And they did, first a
subdued titter and then, as more people saw what was
happening, a ripple of audible laugher. Hazel stopped
short. She reached down and took off the clogs and
walked to the mike carrying them. She held them up
as she spoke into the mike.

"Mr. Webster"—she smiled at the principal, and
then at the audience—"ladies and gentlemen. Do for-
give me. I have never had my clogs amplified before."

The audience burst into a roar of laughter, glad of a chance to do it legitimately.

"I could say I did it on purpose," she said, when they quieted down, "to prove one of the points of my talk, that life is too complicated, too many chains of cause and effect. But actually"—she leaned over and put the clogs on the floor—"I never thought of it." She waited, smiling, till the new wave of laughter died down.

Priscilla caught sight of Peter. He was leaning forward, smiling a little uncertainly, watching Hazel with great intentness. She knew how he felt.

"I'm going to talk a little about transcendental meditation," Hazel was saying, "but I'd like to start out on a personal note, because transcendental meditation is a very personal matter." She paused and Priscilla crossed the fingers of both hands, which were jammed into her pockets. "When I was young, I lived on a farm in Iowa, and one of my best friends was named Rebecca." Again she paused. "Rebecca was a cow." She let the laughter run out. "You think I'm joking, but it's true. The reason I so much enjoyed being with Rebecca was that she seemed to me to have the gift of serenity. Nothing bothered her. Unless of course we were late in milking her. Rebecca had beautiful brown eyes and she would look at me and chew her cud as if she had the answers to all the problems in the world, and had concluded that life was after all a very pleasant affair. I was a tempestuous child, whom everything bothered, so to me Rebecca's calmness was beautiful and much to be envied. After I grew up, it occurred to me that perhaps she was not troubled by problems because she didn't know there were any—a healthy, well-cared-for cow has a pretty even life, after all—but who is to say what the basis was for her outlook on life."

Priscilla looked around. They were listening, at least. Maybe only to laugh, but they were listening. She saw Miss Peterson exchange glances with Mr. Haines, but she couldn't tell what the glance meant.

"Ever since I knew Rebecca, I have searched for peace of mind. It hasn't been easy to find. In the twentieth-century world, we are bedeviled by trivia. Our lives are cluttered with thinginess. (I made that word up. I hope you don't mind.) Hundreds of totally unimportant things push and pull us all day long. Your mother worries about getting you off to school on time, what to have for dinner, whether she has time to clean the house before the guests arrive for tea, whether you are coming down with a cold, whether your father asked her to meet him at the train or not. And you— you worry about whether the teacher is going to call on you for those problems you never got to, or whether you're going to miss the bus, or if that small smear of peanut butter on your sweater shows. And will the club you long to join ask you in, and will you make the team, and will you win the game, and did or did not your mother tell you to be sure to bring home some bread or was it yesterday that she said that?" Hazel looked at them a second. "All right, you say, these things are necessary. They have to be attended to. And they do. But they don't need or deserve the cumulative importance they take on in our lives. They are not the be-all and the end-all of existence. It's when all this takes us over that we lose our tempers, lose our friends, lose our sanity, even sometimes eventually lose our lives. I think there are probably many answers to the question of how to control this situation, how to keep ourselves from falling victim to trivia, and one of those answers is transcendental meditation. Now let me tell you in very basic and oversimplified terms what transcendental meditation is all about."

Priscilla closed her eyes and listened with only half her mind for a few minutes while Hazel went into the explanation, which she had heard from her many times before, of the origin and nature of transcendental meditation. She was telling them about the history of it, about Maharishi Mahesh Yogi, about the goal of "the happiness of absolute awareness."

"It is not a religion." Hazel was leaning forward, her hands on the lectern and her face very earnest now. "It is a way of finding heightened awareness and strengthened stability." She quoted some university researchers who had called it "a fourth state of consciousness characterized by alert restfulness." She explained the levels of ascent as the mind rises above the level of everyday awareness into the pure awareness that is the source of all creative energy and intelligence. "In other words," she said, folding her hands tightly together, "it frees you. It sets you free from your everyday life without canceling it out altogether. People seek a higher level of consciousness in many ways, as you know—some with alcohol, some with drugs, some with frantic activity, some with indiscriminate sex. These are the ways that are dangerous, tempting but dangerous, because they may destroy you.

Meditation will widen your life, not narrow it down to some kind of deadly tunnel vision."

Priscilla looked at the big clock set in the wall at the top of the proscenium. Again she looked quickly at the faces around her. Most of them were listening, but she couldn't tell what they were thinking.

Priscilla hoped Hazel would hear the bell and stop when she was supposed to. Sometimes when she got intent on something she didn't notice anything else.

Hazel was explaining now what the mantra was and how it worked. "Your teacher assigns you your own particular mantra, and a mantra is simply a syllable from the Hindu holy books. It is chosen by the teacher because of its sound, not its meaning." Hazel closed her eyes. "If you allow the mantra to stay in your mind, float in your mind like a bird on a draft of air, all the things and thoughts that have been bothering you will begin to disappear. If you practice this every day"—she opened her eyes—"if you allow your mantra to take over your mind, it too will disappear in time and your mind will move into a new level, a new realm, of awareness. In time, if you are faithful, you may move up from pure awareness to what the Maharishi calls cosmic consciousness, and then to consciousness of God, and at last to a sense of genuine unity with God."

Priscilla moved forward a little so she could see Peter. He had leaned back in his chair and was listening to every word. Peter had always been more interested in the theories that Hazel and Paul talked about than she. Abstractions bothered her. She had to see the specific example before it meant anything to her. For some reason the theme she had written about her grandfather's house came into her mind, and for the first time she understood what the teacher and Jimmy had meant. She, who believed in the concrete, had painted a picture in the abstract.

Hazel had looked at her watch and had offered to answer questions for the rest of the time. No hand went up for a moment, and Priscilla shuddered. They weren't interested. They weren't even going to ask a question. But then one of the mothers at the back of the room asked where one could find a teacher of transcendental meditation, and as soon as Hazel had answered that, at least two dozen hands went up. The principal moved out to the apron of the stage to help pick out the questioners in turn.

A girl asked if the god she was talking about was the Christian god. Hazel explained that it could be any god one believed in.

One of the senior boys asked in an argumentative tone if she had read what John Lennon said about gurus. "He said this Maha-whatever was a waste of time. He said you just decided to be a guru over there, and if you were lucky, you made it, like over here a guy decides to be a pop singer and he turns out like Mick Jagger."

Priscilla felt her face flush with anger at the boy's manner, but Hazel answered him calmly.

"Yes, I have read what John Lennon said. But, you know, nothing works for everybody, does it? Each of us has to find what is best for him. For Mr. Lennon this didn't work; for me it does." She gave him a brief smile and turned to the next questioner.

One of the mothers at the back of the hall asked whether Hazel had taken a course in transcendental meditation.

"Not formally," Hazel said. "I took some lessons from a teacher one summer when we were in Amsterdam. He was an American, as a matter of fact, and he had studied in India with the guru. Neither he nor I were in Amsterdam long enough for me to finish the course. I would like very much to do that if ever we live near enough to one of the centers."

Priscilla remembered that man in Amsterdam. He'd had a full red beard and he had claimed to live on carrot cakes, rice, and tea; but once Priscilla had seen him eating an elaborate curry in one of Amsterdam's Indonesian restaurants.

"There is a course at Harvard," Hazel said, "that I hope to audit in the spring. And the guru has opened a university in Goleta, California. There are a number of centers around the country. One in New York State, I think . . ." She shaded her eyes, peering out into the auditorium. "Peter? Do you remember where it is?"

"In the Catskill Mountains somewhere," Peter said.

The boy sitting next to Peter punched him in the arm playfully and said something that made Peter laugh.

One of Stephanie's friends raised her hand and said, "What's a guru?"

The students laughed.

The girl giggled and looked around as if she had said something witty. "Well, how do I know? I'm just a dumb American."

"A guru is a spiritual teacher," Hazel said.

The girls around the one who had asked the question were laughing and whispering. "Does that make the Reverend Jenkin a guru?" the girl said.

"Jackass," Kath said under her breath. The two students in front of her turned their heads to look at her. They had been writing notes to each other all through Hazel's talk. Kath stared them down, and they went back to their note writing.

"In a sense," Hazel was saying, in answer to the question. "But we don't use that word for our spiritual leaders in this country." She flashed a smile at the principal. "Just as we don't say 'Sahib Webster.'"

Priscilla heard Jimmy Donaldson's laugh behind her. Was he laughing at or with Hazel? She longed for this agony of questioning to stop. She knew a lot of them just wanted to put Hazel on the spot and get a laugh for themselves. She hated them.

"One more question," Mr. Webster said, looking at his watch. He pointed to Miss Peterson's pet, George Fleming. "George?"

Fleming stood up and spoke distinctly in his hoarse voice. "Is it true that most people who go in for these Eastern philosophies and so-called religions are on dope?"

There was complete silence in the hall for a few seconds. Everyone was looking at Hazel.

Then Mr. Webster said, in an annoyed voice, "Fleming, I think Mrs. Parkins has already indicated—"

Hazel held up her hand to stop him. She looked steadily at Fleming and said in a quiet but perfectly audible voice, "No."

The bell rang. Mr. Webster spoke above the hub-
bub of feet scraping on the floor, chairs creaking,
voices. "I am sure we are all grateful to Mrs. Parkins . . ." He raised his arms for silence and failed to
get it. Students at the back were edging toward the
door. He spoke more loudly. ". . . for her very interesting talk." He held his hands high and began to clap.

There was a good deal of applause in the hall, although many students were too busy getting books
and papers together to bother. Jimmy Donaldson
stood up, clapping hard, and shouted "Bravo!" Some
of the others, including Kath, joined him. But it was
hard to tell who was on his feet to applaud and who
was just trying to get out of his row of seats. Priscilla
didn't know whether she ought to clap or not. She
tried to see Peter for a clue, but he was lost in the
milling crowd. She decided to clap anyway, a little bit.

Over the heads of the students, she could just see
Hazel, smiling. Then Hazel and Mr. Webster left the
stage, Hazel carrying her clogs. Priscilla sighed and got
up. She was limp with relief that it was over. She
wished she could go home.

Jimmy leaned toward her and said above the din,
"She's great!"

She gave him an uncertain smile. It was nice of him
to say it. And Kath, too. Kath, her eyes shining the
way they did when she really liked something, said,
"Oh, I love your mother."

But they were her friends. She would probably never
know what the other kids really thought about Hazel's
talk. She tried to imagine Mrs. Wentworth giving a
lecture on such a subject. It was inconceivable. But

when she said that later to Kath, as a kind of joke, Kath looked at her in surprise.

"Mrs. Wentworth gave a very good talk last year on horse breeding."

"Well, horse breeding, yes. That's what people are interested in."

Kath looked puzzled. "I think a lot more kids are interested in Zen and transcendental meditation and that kind of thing than they are in raising horses. How many people raise horses?" She smiled at Priscilla as they went into study hall. "You're just in a state of shock because you were nervous. But it was great, Pris. Your mother was great. They loved her."

"I hope so," Priscilla said. She was thinking of Stephanie's friend and Fleming and the senior boy.

Stephanie went past her desk and said, "Hey, Priscilla, don't forget the slumber party. My house at seven."

"I won't forget." As if she could forget. She began to make a list of what she should take. Pajamas and robe, slippers, toothbrush, toothpaste . . . Should she take her own towel? She had never stayed overnight at another girl's house. She turned to Kath to ask her about the towel, but Kath had her head bent over her Latin book, frowning over Cicero. Maybe it wouldn't be tactful to ask Kath, since she hadn't been invited. Maybe Hazel would know. It was hard to imagine Hazel at a slumber party, but she said she had been to one or two, years ago.

It was raining hard when school let out. Mr. Puddleford was there in his new Ford to pick up Kath. He waited for Priscilla, beckoning to her urgently, rain streaming down his broad face as he leaned out the window. He was still in his good suit.

All the way home he talked about the rise in prices in food for the school cafeteria. Even in his best clothes, he smelled of grease.

"Can't keep up with it," he kept saying. "Can't get the taxpayers to realize we need more money when prices go up. Darned school needs more money, no two ways about it." He drove as near to the castle as he could get and said, "There you are, young lady. Run between the raindrops."

"Thank you very much."

"Don't mention it." Just before the door closed, he called to her, "That mother of yours is all right."

Priscilla looked back in surprise, but he was already pulling the car around in a tight circle on the wet grass. Kath waved. Priscilla stood there a moment in the rain, watching them go. She wondered what Mr. Puddleford had got out of Hazel's talk. She tried to think of him sitting cross-legged and meditating. It made her laugh, though she had gotten rather fond of Mr. Puddleford. She ran for the house as a squally wind blew rain in her face. Hazel's talk was over, and now she could concentrate on the slumber party. Should she take a towel?

TWENTY-ONE

JOURNAL: What a day. Or even more so, what a night. What is the sense of trying to do things right when it turns out wrong? Paul took Hazel to Essex for a fried clam dinner because, as he said, she'd given such a good performance at the school. Mr. Puddleford told him so. I love fried clams more than life itself, but I couldn't go because they wouldn't get me back in time for the slumber party. Peter was working late. I forgot to ask Hazel about the towel. Anyway, she and Paul were so full of things to talk about. Some of the PTA women had asked her if she would conduct a class in transcendental meditation. Paul thinks she should do it, but she keeps saying she doesn't know enough. He says she does. She asked me if I thought the talk went all right, and I said sure. I didn't tell her I heard some mean cracks, like when Mrs. Adams asked her social studies class (the seniors) what message they got from Hazel's talk, and Phil Donovan said, "Buy a cow." Everybody thought it was hilarious, and I heard it repeated about eight times. Paul said Mr. Puddleford told him the Board of Selectmen got some complaints because Paul did some building here without a permit. I can tell Paul is worried. So, anyway, I walked over to Stephanie's at a quarter of seven. I wasn't sure how long it would take and I didn't want to be early, so I walked all around the Town Hall and down toward Ipswich before I went to the house. Then I was late.

They have a nice house with a big sun room full of plants. Stephanie's mother looks like Mrs. Onassis, and her father is about seven feet tall. They have a Persian cat named Frederick. I kept worrying about Hassan. He was sad about being left home alone. I almost asked Kath to come and sit with him, but that seemed kind of ridiculous.

There were five other girls at Stephanie's. I know them all vaguely but I never talked to them before, really. They were sitting around in what they call the family room, which is in the basement, eating potato chips and jam sandwiches and drinking Coke. There was a fire in the fireplace. I thought it was going to be nice, but right away I felt strange. They stopped talking when I came in, and when they started again, it sounded funny, kind of strained, as if I'd walked in when they were talking about me. Peter would say I was paranoid. Maybe so, but you can tell.

Stephanie's mother made her take me upstairs to one of the bedrooms to put my bag down and all. I had a flight bag from SAS, and Stephanie acted like she'd never seen a flight bag before. She made me open it up and when she saw the towel, she gave me a funny look and said, "Did you think we didn't have any towels?" So I'd done the wrong thing there. She took out my robe and looked it all over and said, "Hey, neat!" as if she really thought it was weird. It's a perfectly ordinary brushed wool robe I got in Stockholm last year. There's nothing wrong with it. It's blue.

When we went downstairs, four kids were playing Monopoly and the others were arguing over what to put on the stereo. They ended up with hard rock, very loud. I like rock, but we've never been allowed to play it loud like that because Hazel says it can damage your hearing. I didn't know what to do with myself. They were talking about boys, and I didn't have much to contribute. Let's face it: I didn't have ANYTHING to contribute. Mrs. Wheeler brought us some popcorn, and Mr. Wheeler yelled at Stephanie to turn down the stereo. She made a face and turned it down, and five minutes later she turned it up again. She said they would be going out pretty soon and we wouldn't have to worry about them. Once I looked up and saw Mr. Wheeler standing in the doorway with a drink in his hand, looking at us as if we were freaks. Peter says a lot of parents are really cut off from their kids. I'm glad ours aren't.

Then the Wheelers went out. Stephanie got a bottle of her father's sherry and we all had some. I don't really like it but I drank it and it made me feel weird. I think it might be the sherry that made me do what I did, but I don't know. I might have done it anyway. Here's what it was. The kids were all lying around on the sofas and on the floor, talking away about this boy and that boy, and sometimes about other girls. They made fun of some of the girls they don't like. I kept thinking if I wasn't Peter's sister, I'd have been a subject of conversation instead of a guest. But I have to admit, if I felt like that, I shouldn't have gone to the party in the first place. They asked me a lot of questions about Peter, who he dated, who he liked, and all that. I said I didn't know who he liked, and he didn't date much because he worked and he didn't have much time. They really pestered me about what he thought of Stephanie and other girls. They never mentioned Hazel's speech, except that one of them asked me where she got the clogs. This girl wanted some clogs like those. They asked me what European boys were like, and since I'd been such a failure so far, I made up a few stories about Hans, a boy I'd worshiped from afar when we were in the Rhineland, and I threw in a few hints about how exciting Finnish boys were. Then somehow, about ten o'clock somebody mentioned Kath. It was a kid I really don't like, a kid named Brenda something (Peter calls her Brenda Starr). She had had the most sherry and I think she was a little potted. Anyway, she said Kath was a dumb ox.

I was feeling kind of brave from the sherry, and I said, "You're out of your mind," in quite a loud voice. They all looked at me.

Stephanie said, "Oh, that's right, she's a friend of yours." And she laughed, but she gave Brenda a warning look.

Brenda wasn't about to be warned off. "How could she be anybody's friend?" she said. "Unless maybe a cow." And they all screamed with laughter, because I knew they were thinking of Phil Donovan's crack about Hazel's speech.

I said, "You should be so dumb. She's an honor student."

"Well," Brenda said in her drawly voice, "if your idea of personality and charm is the ability to conjugate a Latin verb . . ."

Somebody said, "I can do that—*amo, amas, amat.*"

"Kath is just like her father," Brenda said. "She'll look just like him in a few years."

"There's nothing wrong with Mr. Puddleford." My face was so hot, I felt as if I had a fever. "He's good enough to be on the school board and the Board of Selectmen . . ."

"And live on a king's grant," Stephanie said, laughing.

"He looks like Henry the Eighth," Brenda said. She liked it because people were laughing. "I saw a movie about Henry the Eighth. Eating. He'd pick up this half a sheep . . ." She sat up and grabbed a needlepoint footstool and pretended to gnaw on it. "Umm! Yum! Good! I can see Mr. Puddleford and Kath at each end of the table, tearing away at a whole roast with their bare teeth, throwing the bones on the floor . . ."

"And that stupid little Mrs. Puddleford picking up the bones," Stephanie said. They were all laughing fit to kill themselves.

"And they get fatter and fatter and fatter . . ."

I stood up. I said, "Stop it." I guess I said it pretty loud, because they all looked up surprised. I began to shake, I was so furious. "Kath Puddleford is my best friend," I said. "You're not going to sit here and insult my best friend. Or her father and mother either."

"Oh, come on, Priscilla," Stephanie said. She looked annoyed.

"I mean it. I won't listen to it," I said.

"Then why don't you go home, where you won't have to?" Brenda said. She tipped up the sherry bottle and let the last drops fall on her tongue.

"All right," I said. "I will." I ran out of the room and upstairs. I had to go to the bedroom to get my coat and my bag, though it would have been more effective if I could have just stormed right out.

And I made it worse by barging into the wrong bedroom, Stephanie's mother's room. I was just coming out of it when Stephanie came up the stairs. She gave me a funny look, as if I was probably looting the family jewels or something.

I always say something really stupid when I'm in a rage, and this was no exception. I said, "Why don't you keep your darned bedrooms where they belong?" And I tore into the opposite room and got my things.

"Listen," Stephanie said, "you'd better not go home."

"Why not?"

"My mother will be wild."

"Tell her I had a sudden attack of the plague." I pushed past her and went out, slamming the front door.

It had stopped raining earlier in the day, but it was very dark, no stars. I stood on the sidewalk a minute, pulling myself together. I could imagine what a big laugh they were having. They'd be glad I'd left because now they could discuss the Parkinses.

I walked out to the main road, near the Town Hall, and started toward home. I wasn't too happy about walking all that way in the pitch dark, but Paul and Hazel probably wouldn't be home yet, and on Fridays Peter worked till eleven. I walked down past the entrance to the Wentworth house and past Jimmy Donaldson's house. I could see the lights in the Donaldson house, and I wished I was in either one of them. Those kids didn't mention Jimmy once when they were discussing boys. I was glad. That meant he didn't bother with them.

After half a mile or so, I sat down on the stone wall for a minute, just to think. The granite rocks felt cold. The whole world seemed cold, and I began to wonder if I was always going to be looking in at other people's lighted houses. Then I decided I was feeling too darned sorry for myself. I had a wonderful, good family that loved me and never yelled at me, practically, and I had a good friend like Kath, and Jimmy was my friend, and even Anne Wentworth a little bit. Though I had to admit Anne was more like an acquaintance. And I had Hassan. I stood up and started home, walking fast, because I'd remembered how lonesome Hassan was.

When I came across the field to our house, I could have cried for joy. Paul's truck was in the grass. The lights in the castle were on, the soft, yellow light of the kerosine lamp, looking warm and cozy. And Hassan ran out to greet me, almost knocking me over. We ran like mad for the castle, and we burst in, and there were Paul and Hazel sitting in front of the fire reading. They looked surprised. Hazel said, "Prissy. What's the matter?" And I said, "Nothing's the matter. I love you and I'm the luckiest girl in the whole world." And I burst into tears.

TWENTY-TWO

As Hazel had predicted, after the slumber party fiasco, Priscilla found the whole thing didn't really make much difference. For once she felt quite sure that she had done the right thing, and she got the idea that some of the other girls thought so too, though she was sure they would never say so. Although Brenda and two of her followers made a point of ignoring Priscilla entirely, the others, even Stephanie, still behaved much as they had before the party, speaking to her but never stopping to talk. But the really surprising thing was that she didn't care whether they were friendly or not. They had stopped being important to her.

There were other things to think of. For one thing, the weather had turned cold and the ice in the river was thick enough for skating. Priscilla loved to skate, and now almost every afternoon she went up and down the river from the old stone bridge, up where "the back road" crossed the river, down to the edge of the old Haverhill farm. Often Hazel joined her, sometimes Kath, and on weekends Peter and Paul.

And one day at school when she mentioned skating to Jimmy, he asked her if he could come too. He was a fast, skillful skater, and the two of them flew up and down the river, hands crossed. One Friday when the band was not playing anywhere, he asked her to go with him to the movies in Ipswich. Priscilla had a very good time, and they did it several more times when Jimmy had a free weekend night. Afterward, Jimmy always came in, and Hazel would make hot chocolate and cheese sandwiches toasted over the open fire. It pleased Priscilla that her family liked Jimmy and that he liked them. The mutual admiration between Hazel and Jimmy was especially strong. Priscilla liked to say that when her mother was there, Jimmy forgot all about whose date he was. He loved to discuss philosophy and religion with both Hazel and Paul, and he often took home one of Paul's books to read.

One night after he had gone, and Priscilla was lying on the wolfskin rug with her head pillowed on Hassan's shoulder, Hazel said, "How wonderful it is, Pris, that you've found friends like Kath and Jimmy. I guess we were selfish, but I never quite realized what we were keeping you from in Europe. You *are* happier here."

"Even if we didn't make it to Surrey," Peter said. He grinned at Priscilla over the top of his book.

Paul looked up from a piece of wood he was carving for a chair back. He exchanged glances with Hazel, and then he said, "I think we're due for a small family conference."

Priscilla felt a stab of alarm. Family conferences meant something serious. "Is it about the permits to fix this place?" Although she had tried to put it out of her mind, the woman who ran the dry goods store had stopped her downtown one day and said in her hypocritical do-gooder's voice, "I heard you folks are going to be turned out of that shelter you've got up there on Willow Lane." And when Priscilla had looked shocked, she had gone on, "Well, that's the way it goes. People don't have respect for property like they used to, but it still carries weight, you know. You can't fool with property."

When Priscilla had reported the puzzling remarks at home, Paul had said quickly, "Don't listen to her. She was telling everybody that Hazel was a godless heathen, after her talk at school, and I'm afraid I told her off. She's just nursing her grudge."

Now he said, "No. I do have to go before the Board of Selectmen next week but I'll cross that bridge when I come to it. What I wanted to tell you children was, I had a letter from Jason, in Surrey . . ." He stopped and looked at Priscilla.

"Something has happened to the house," she said. She tightened her arm around Hassan, who groaned softly in his sleep.

"I'm afraid so, Prissy."

"It burned." She had a vivid image of the house she loved, the house of her forefathers, blazing against a cold Maine sky.

"No," Paul said gently, "it just collapsed. They had some bad northeast gales, and it just . . . fell down." His dark eyes looked at her sadly.

"We can put it back up when we get up there, can't we?" She couldn't bear to think of it lying in a heap of rubble, the little "sitting room" with the small-paned windows that looked out to sea, the enormous brick fireplace, the big, sunny kitchen, her own little room that Grandfather said had been her father's . . . And the hollyhocks all torn down. "We can rebuild it. You always said those old houses are so solid."

Paul shook his head. "Jason said a lot of the wood had rotted. Riddled with wood worm, he said. A lot of those big timbers just crumbled."

Priscilla looked down at Hassan's silky head. It was like hearing that somebody you loved had died; you felt numb, but there wasn't any pain yet. Like a tooth just before the Novocain wears off.

"Then we can't even use the lumber to build a new house," Peter said.

"Oh, some of it is probably still sound. We'd have to check it out."

"It's still standing in your memory, Pris," Hazel said softly. "You'll never lose that house in your mind. Change comes to everything except the memories we carry in our heads."

Suddenly the pain began, perhaps because Hazel was talking about the house as if it were really gone forever. Priscilla got to her feet. "I don't want a memory," she said. "I want my grandfather's house." She went to her room and lay down on her bed. Without seeing it she stared at the design Paul had carved into the headboard. Hassan came in sleepily and curled up with his neck curved to match the curve of her knees. He lifted his head and laid his long black muzzle across her leg.

She lay still for a long time, remembering the house in different situations, in morning sunshine, in a lashing rainstorm, lit up by lightning, washed down with the blown salt mist of the sea. She re-created in her mind the way it smelled, a mixture of old wood, long ago potpourris, mothballs, fish chowder cooking, pine trees. She thought of the way it creaked and rattled in the wind, the thunk of an occasional brick falling from one of the chimneys, the rasp of the iron hinges on the front door.

"Well," she said to Hassan at last, "the lodestone can't fix that one, can it. All the king's horses and all the queen's lodestones can't put my house together again." But she didn't cry. She just lay quietly, hollow with a sense of loss.

For some time she couldn't speak to anyone about it, but one cold, sunny afternoon as she and Jimmy crouched on their skates under the old stone bridge to catch their breath before they started back, she told him. He listened without speaking, and she found herself going on about what the house had meant to her. "I suppose you think it's crazy to care," she said, "you people who have had the same house for centuries." She was thinking of Anne Wentworth.

"Nothing like that is crazy," Jimmy caught hold of the cold wet rocks above his head. "This is supposed to be one of the oldest bridges in North America. I guess some day it will be torn down, to widen the road or some stupid thing, and there will go a part of history we've been able to look at and touch."

She looked up at the bridge. "I didn't know it was that old." A car crossed the bridge, and the stones rumbled. "I'd rather hear a wagon crossing it," she said. "Wouldn't that be nice?"

"I guess wagons made quite a racket too. I don't know how far back you have to go to find the 'good old days.' Maybe right back to the time life started on earth. But I wouldn't like that too much, would you?" He smiled at her. "I mean who wants to be an amoeba?"

"You mean there never was a good time?"

He shrugged. "Or else whatever good there is is always available."

"You've been talking to my family too much. You're getting to sound like them."

He laughed. "Is that bad?"

She found herself telling him the story of Titania's lodestone. She had never told anyone before because she thought it made Hazel sound like some kind of nut. But Jimmy would never think that. When she finished, he didn't say anything. He took off one skate, cleared the slush from the blade, and put it on again. He laced it up carefully. He was a person whose shoe-string never came untied.

"Of course it was just a nice family fairy tale," she said, "but when you grow out of all those myths, it's kind of a shock."

He reached down to help her to her feet. They had to crouch until they were out of the low arch of the bridge. Then he looked at her, the wind reddening his cheeks, and his eyes looking bright behind his glasses. "You wish you still believed in the lodestone, don't you?" he asked. He held out his mittened hands for hers and stroked off down the river before she could answer. And she was glad, because she would not have known what to say.

TWENTY-THREE

Paul had finally been asked to appear before the Board of Selectmen on a Friday evening. Anne Wentworth had invited Priscilla and Peter and her cousin Jimmy to come skating on the big pond below the Wentworth house while the meeting was going on. Priscilla was torn between excitement over going to the Wentworths', where she had not been before, and worry over the outcome of the Selectmen's meeting.

"Why worry?" Peter said. "That won't change anything. I think the Wentworths are asking us to get our minds off it, so let's relax and enjoy it."

Mrs. Wentworth had already left for the meeting herself when Paul and Hazel left Priscilla and Peter at the driveway to the Wentworth house.

"Jimmy said he would bring you home," Hazel said. She looked serene, not at all as if she might be about to lose a home she had worked hard for. "Have a good time, loves, and don't forget to thank the Wentworths. It was thoughtful of them."

Priscilla leaned on Paul's door. "It's going to be all right, isn't it? They won't take the castle away from us?"

He gave her a reassuring smile. "Titania has her lodestone with her."

They stood watching the red taillight of the pickup as it bumped down the road toward the Town Hall. "I'm scared," Priscilla said.

"We'll put a hex on things if we worry about them." Peter slung his skates over his shoulder and started down the graveled driveway.

"Kath told me that dry goods woman has been telling everybody we're squatters, atheists and all sorts of wild things. What has she got against us anyway?"

"Myrtle at the Paper Store says she is the self-appointed conscience of the town. Not that Myrt put it quite that way . . ." He chuckled.

"Well, I don't believe one woman can get us evicted."

"The trouble is, Myrt says, the woman thinks she's right . . . You know, on the side of God. Myrt says one day she saw her smash a bottle of paregoric that poor old Angie Withrow had gone clear to Salem to get. In a way she was right, of course. I mean Angie shouldn't be swigging all that paregoric, but why did the old bag have to be all that cruel. Myrt said Angie fell in a heap on the sidewalk and cried like a baby."

They passed the big paddock and moved along the frost-hard road toward the house. Priscilla was looking at it curiously. She hadn't seen it close up before. It was a big, whitewashed brick house with two wings. "What a pretty house," she said.

"Myrt says during World War II that dry goods woman's mother used to go to Boston every day for months to protest at the State House about drivers of beer trucks getting gas coupons. I guess righteousness runs in the family." Peter stepped up to the big brass knocker and gave it a thump.

Almost at once Anne opened the door. She looked much better than she had. The mononucleosis was cleared up, and after Christmas vacation she would be going back to school. "Hi, mates," she said. "Come along in."

She took their coats and piled them up on a chair in the hall and led them into a large living room. Jimmy was there. He came toward Priscilla at once, his face lighting up. But Priscilla hardly saw him, because standing with feet apart, back to the fireplace, was Hollister, obviously home for the weekend. He was talking to another young man who lay stretched out on the floor with a can of beer balanced on his chest. Anne took her guests up to her brother.

"Holly, you've met Peter Parkins . . ." She waited while the two shook hands. "This is his sister Priscilla."

Vaguely Priscilla heard Anne go on to say that the young man on the floor, who now struggled to his feet, was Hollister's roommate, Vin Kerry. She could not have said what Vin Kerry looked like, although she acknowledged the introduction. All she was aware of was Hollister Wentworth. He was wearing a pair of Oxford gray slacks and a blue turtleneck sweater, and to Priscilla he was almost too attractive to be a living human being. She tried to sound casual and offhand when she said she was glad to meet him, but it seemed to her that everyone in the room must know what a momentous event it was. And especially he himself must know. He smiled at her, but she was dismayed to see that it was the kind of smile big brothers give their sisters' friends. He saw her as a child. She wanted to say to him, "Just you wait. In a couple or three years you won't look at me like that. You'll see me."

She was aware suddenly of Jimmy, who was asking her if she wanted to go skating or not. He sounded impatient, which was not like Jimmy.

"Yes, of course," she said.

Anne was showing Peter her collection of cassette cartridges. He was admiring her new cassette player and going on about Dolby decoders or something as if he really knew what he was talking about. Well, Priscilla thought, perhaps he does. It was being brought to her attention more and more lately that things went on in people's heads that didn't necessarily show. Her own, for instance.

"I meant to tell you to bring your dog," Anne said to Priscilla, when at last they had all, except Hollister and Vin, gotten their coats, mittens, scarves and skates together. She lowered her voice. "He'd be safe here."

"He's guarding the castle," Peter said. "It's under siege, you know."

Jimmy, his good nature restored as they went out and left Hollister behind, said, "It shall never be taken. We'll man the ramparts. Pull up the drawbridge. Pollute the moat."

They ran down the drive toward the pond, past the stable, past the kennel where Mrs. Wentworth's corgis set up a clamor. The pond was a big dark oval in the evening setting of willow trees and birches. There was a small three-sided hut where Anne said they sometimes cooked a meal, and there were benches for changing into skates.

With Jimmy's expert help, Priscilla was the first one out on the ice. She could see the white dust where skates had been. Jimmy found a broom in the hut and skated fast up and down the pond, sweeping.

Anne looked over Peter's shoulder and laughed. "Look at him. The Sorcerer's Apprentice."

There was a cold three-quarter moon overhead, and the stars seemed unusually close and bright. A light wind tingled their faces and made them glow. They skated for a long time, stopping now and then to get their breath and to talk a few minutes. Priscilla thought she had never had a better time in her life. If only Hollister had come out and if only Hassan were there, it would have been perfect.

Trying to sound casual, she said to Anne, "Does your brother skate?"

"Oh yes," Anne said, "and he's disgustingly good at it, the way he is at everything. But he won't skate with my friends, of course. He's a big college man."

"Oh, Holly isn't that bad," Jimmy said. "After all, he *is* nineteen."

"My mother is forty-three," Anne said, "but she enjoys being with my friends." But she didn't sound really angry with her brother.

After a while Jimmy and Peter built a fire in the shed, and they all crouched close to it to get warm.

"I feel like a baked Alaska," Jimmy said, "part of me's ice cold, part of me's hot." He took off his mittens and held Priscilla's hands toward the fire. "Your hands are cold, lady."

They stayed close to the fire for about half an hour, talking and joking. Priscilla was trying hard to think only about the present moment. She particularly didn't want to think about what was going on at the Town Hall. She was sure she could not bear losing the castle and having to move on again, just when she had begun to feel settled. Even the loss of the house in Surrey didn't seem quite so awful now, if they could stay here.

On the walk back she was quiet, looking at the house in the darkness, trying to imagine what it would be like to live in a place that had been in your family for so long. She had had a taste of what it would be like, but now her house was gone. I'm thinking in circles, she thought, and then it occurred to her that if you could find a place that had the right vibrations for you, as the castle did, even if your own old place was gone perhaps you could bring to the new one what you had found in the old. Like transplanting a plant. Only you had to do it carefully and lovingly, tamp the earth all around it . . .

"Here comes Mother," Anne said, as the Rover's headlights came down the drive.

And suddenly Priscilla wanted to run and hide. She was terrified of what the news might be about the castle. She grabbed Peter's hand and felt his answering pressure. It didn't mean to him what it meant to her, but he was sympathizing with her.

Anne ran forward as the car stopped and the door opened. "Mother, how did it turn out?"

Priscilla held her breath while Mrs. Wentworth came around the front of the car toward them. She was smiling. "It's all right."

TWENTY-FOUR

THEY sat around the big fireplace in the Went-worth living room and ate sandwiches and drank cocoa while Mrs. Wentworth told them about the meeting with the Board of Selectmen.

"Your mother and father were marvelous," she said to Priscilla and Peter. "They're so original and so . . . well, sincere, I think almost everyone was with them. Poor Jessie made one of her impassioned speeches but it never really took."

"Jessie is a nut," Anne said.

"Well, she seems to interpret Scriptures in her own way. Instead of 'If thine eye offend thee, pluck it out,' she seems to read it, 'If your eye offend me, I'll pluck it out.' She's perfectly sincere, poor soul."

"I don't understand," Priscilla said, "how one person could stir up such a fuss. I mean she's not even on the Board of Selectmen, is she?"

"No, I suppose it's just that a persuasive talker can always stir things up if she—or he—puts her mind to it. She buttonholes people, you see. Anne dear, give Peter some more cocoa."

"Hollister says she uses the stranger-within-our-gates principle," Anne said. She reached for Peter's cup. Jimmy got up and put another log on the fire and then stood with his elbow on the mantel, looking at Priscilla.

"What does that mean?"

"Oh, you know, stirring people up against outsiders. I guess you can always do that."

"Outsiders?" Priscilla felt dismayed. She didn't want to be an outsider here. She had come a long way to be at home.

"Hollister has just caught a bad case of the academic ailment," Mrs. Wentworth said. "He's learned what fun it is to put everybody in a category."

"But do people still think of us as outsiders?" Priscilla asked.

"Well, Pris, we really are," Peter said. "We're the people from over the water, as Myrt says."

Mrs. Wentworth saw Priscilla's distress. "To most of us, you are certainly not strangers, Priscilla," she said. "To us you are neighbors and friends. But there are always some people everywhere who can be appealed to on that 'we' and 'them' basis, unfortunately. If you come from over the town line, you're a stranger to them. I suppose it's the oldest form of snobbery there is, and certainly the most idiotic."

"I'm a stranger in Ipswich," Jimmy said. "I'm an outlander in Salem. When our group plays out of town, we're always 'the Naumkeag bunch.' It's just the way people are."

"Anyway," Mrs. Wentworth went on, "your father told them what he had done at the castle, and they asked him how much he had spent and so on. Of course the question of permits arose, why hadn't he applied for permits. He disarmed them completely by saying, 'I was afraid you wouldn't let me have them.'"

"Oh, dear!" Priscilla said. Paul's passion for telling the truth always scared her. Couldn't he have bent it just a little?

"Of course they had to pretend to disapprove. They frowned and talked about the illegalities and the necessity of fines and whether he should be allowed to stay on. Then Mr. Puddleford spoke up, and he was splendid. He gave your father such a glowing character report."

"And Mr. Puddleford belongs," Peter said with a touch of irony.

"Oh, my yes. There's been a Puddleford since time began in this town."

"Did my mother have to speak?" Priscilla asked.

"My dear, she provided the *coup de grace*. She told them about her phone call to Sally, which I had witnessed, of course . . ."

Priscilla looked at Peter, but he shook his head blankly. "What phone call?"

"She didn't tell you? Oh, she was probably afraid it wouldn't work. She came over here this morning and hatched a little plan with me. She called Sally long distance—pure luck getting her, and of course it was an ungodly hour there—but she asked Sally if she would write the Board that she approved of the improvements you've all made and that she agreed to a lease.

Well, knowing Sally, I knew she'd love the idea of a lease, steady money coming in, but I was afraid she'd forget about writing or it wouldn't come in time to do any good or something, so I got on the phone and persuaded her to call the Town Hall right then. She did, you see, and it worked."

Peter threw back his head and laughed. "Titania's lodestone."

"After your mother told them about calling Sally, Bernie Haskell read off the details of the conversation he'd had with Sally, and that did it. Jessie and her friends couldn't claim anymore that you were—what was that dreadful word they used?—'squatters.'"

Priscilla felt tremendously relieved, but she was still shaken by the idea that a number of people in town thought of them as enemies and intruders. She spoke of it to Jimmy and Peter, when Jimmy was driving them home.

"Priscilla, you can't expect one hundred percent joyful acceptance from everybody, anywhere," Jimmy said. "Nobody gets that. Look at the Wentworths: they've been here forever, but a lot of people detest them because they've got a lot of money. They say Aunt Anna is a snob and all that. And what they say about my father, you wouldn't believe. He's been sued for malpractice, he's been threatened, he's had nasty anonymous letters, and he's probably the most gossiped-about man in town except the rector."

"Your father?" Priscilla was shocked.

"Sure. The more you're in the public eye, the worse you get it. You're in the public eye a little right now because you're new in town. Just don't worry about it."

"When will we stop being new?" Priscilla asked.

Jimmy laughed. "Possibly when your great-grand-children are born in your castle." He turned in at the Puddleford drive and then cut across the field toward the castle. "Anyway you've just won your first battle. You've kept your nifty house."

"Come on in," Peter said. "It's still early."

"Just for a minute. I want to congratulate your mother and father."

Priscilla ran ahead of them, calling Hassan. One of her worries had been whether, if they had to give up the castle, they could keep Hassan.

He didn't come bounding out as he usually did. She opened the door, which was slightly ajar, and went in. Kath was there, and she looked as if she had been crying. Paul and Hazel were both standing up and they didn't seem happy, as she had expected. "What is it?" she said. She looked around. "Where's Hassan?"

Kath spoke. She was almost in tears. "It's my fault, Priscilla."

"No, it isn't, Kath," Hazel said.

Priscilla felt her chest tighten. "What is? Where's Hassan?"

"We don't know, Pris," Paul said. "Kath heard him barking, after we left. She came over to see if he was all right . . ." He looked at Kath.

"First I thought I heard a car up on the road," Kath said. "Then Hassan barking a lot. I came over to check, the way I always do if you're gone. He seemed excited or scared. He dashed out past me when I opened the door, and he took off up toward the old bridge. I've hunted and hunted, Priscilla, and I can't find him." Tears filled her eyes.

Priscilla swallowed. "Don't worry, Kath. He'll come back. Of course it wasn't your fault." She put her hand on Kath's arm. "Don't worry." But she felt sick with anxiety. He never ran off like that. What could have happened?

"Let's all go hunt," Jimmy said. "I've got a big flashlight in the car. I'll take the riverbank up as far as the bridge. Pete, why don't you cover the road." He found a piece of paper and a pencil and made a rough map. "I know you've probably been all over this, Kath, but we'll keep going till we find him. He's bound to be around here somewhere."

Kath looked at Jimmy gratefully and nodded.

"Give us a territory too, Jimmy," Hazel said.

Priscilla watched Jimmy as he gave directions, but her mind was far away. She was trying to think the way Hassan would think. He was not a dog that scared easily. What could have upset him? She wondered if he'd gotten frightened about being in the house alone. It didn't seem likely. He had stayed alone before with nothing more than a look of longing when she left. And Kath almost always came by to see that he was all right. There couldn't have been anything in the house to scare him. Kath said she thought she had heard a car, but Hassan wasn't afraid of cars, though he sometimes barked when he heard one.

She took a flashlight from her father and followed the course Jimmy had given her, down the river and around the back of the Puddleford farm. She walked along the edge of the river ice. It was slippery, but it saved time because she didn't have to make her way through the thick brush on the bank. "Hassan," she called. "Hassan, boy." But all she could hear was the voices of the others, moving away from her, calling "Hassan."

TWENTY-FIVE

THAT night, long after the searchers had given up, the first snow of the season fell. Priscilla, lying wide awake in her bed, saw the flakes brush gently against her window. She got up for the dozenth time and went to make sure that the front door was ajar, so Hassan could get in if he came home in the night. A small heap of dry flakes had already fallen in the little, triangular space left by the slightly opened door. Priscilla opened the door wider and felt the snow fall lightly on her face, smelled the dampish unmistakable smell of new snow. Her spirits lifted a little. If Hassan were anywhere around, they could find his footprints now, when it stopped snowing.

She moved away from the cold doorway to the window, pressing her face against the cold glass. Hassan, Hassan, Hassan, come back. And the name that had been in her mind ever since she had found him gone now surfaced and wouldn't be talked down. Sonny Detheridge. The car that Kath had heard must have belonged to Sonny Detheridge. He had probably heard somewhere that his dog or a dog like his had been seen on the Weston place. He had come looking for him. Hassan had recognized the sound of the car (he always recognized Paul's truck, long before it was in sight) and he had been frightened. When he bolted, he had either gone clear off where nobody could find him—as he had probably done when he ran away from the kennel—or else Sonny Detheridge had seen him and picked him up. After all, it *was* his dog. That was why she had tried not to let herself admit that this was probably what had happened. If it was, she was helpless. Hassan belonged to Sonny Detheridge, not to her. He wasn't stealing her dog, he was just catching his own dog.

But at least she would have to find out. She couldn't go on pretending the dog was just lost, when he was probably right now in a kennel in Pride's Crossing. She would have to go and see.

She lingered a little longer, watching the slow spiraling swirl of flakes catching on the trees, softening the outlines of the stone walls, whitening the ivy. She wondered if Hassan liked to play in the snow. She had looked forward to romping with him when the snow came. She straightened up. If she stood here thinking of things like that, she'd end up in tears.

The next morning, Saturday, she got up even before the usual time and had breakfast with Paul. She told her parents what she thought about Sonny Detheridge.

Hazel nodded. "I was thinking that, too. We had better go over there and find out."

"I agree," Paul said. "Drop me off at work and drive over to Pride's." He put his hand on Priscilla's head for a second. "It won't do much good, I'm afraid, except to satisfy your mind. I mean, it *is* Detheridge's dog, in all probability. When I heard he was back, I knew we'd have to tell him about Hassan, but I guess I kept putting it off." He shook his head, frowning. "I liked that dog."

"Well, don't speak of him in the past tense," Hazel said. "He's still Hassan." She went into the bedroom to change from her robe to jeans and sweater. Peter was still asleep, so she left him a note.

The snow had stopped, the sun was out, and the world was white. Even the old pickup looked better. "Our silver chariot," Hazel said. She patted the door, and a cloud of light snow drifted with the air current.

When Paul got out at the garage, he kissed Priscilla on the cheek. "Good luck, baby, but don't hope for too much. One of these days maybe I'll get enough money together to buy you an Afghan." Then he added quickly, "I know, honey. It's Hassan you love."

Mr. Puddleford came hurrying out of the garage to ask if the dog had been found. "Kath told me about it. Listen, if you feel Kath is responsible—"

They all interrupted him. "Mr. Puddleford," Priscilla said, "Kath was doing us a favor. One reason I always felt it was safe to leave Hassan was I knew Kath would check up on him. *Don't* let her think it's her fault."

He pushed his cap back on his head. "All right. I'll tell her. She's taking it hard."

Hazel asked Mr. Puddleford where exactly the kennel was, and he gave her the directions, drawing a little map in the snow on the truck so she could see.

"Put it on paper for you if you say so."

Hazel shook her head. "I've got it." She smiled at him. "Thank you again for all you did at the meeting. We appreciate it."

Mr. Puddleford laughed. "Purely selfish motives, madam. You don't think I was going to stand still and let them take away my best man? Best darned man I ever had." He stood back and waved his cap at them as they drove off.

"People are awfully good," Hazel said.

"Some of them," Priscilla said.

The drive to Pride's Crossing was slow. The streets were slushy with the melting snow, and traffic was moving cautiously. Hazel found the lane with the sign that said PRIDE'S KENNELS, AFGHANS AND SALUKIS, SONNY DETHERIDGE. DRIVE SLOW.

It had once been an estate. The grounds were spacious, and there was a small gate cottage now boarded up. Hazel drove slowly along the winding drive, past an unused tennis court, until she came to the kennels. Priscilla was leaning forward trying to see the dogs that were out in their runs. There were about ten of them, a few Salukis and the rest Afghans.

"The runs are too short for those big dogs," she said. She couldn't see Hassan anywhere.

Hazel parked, and they got out. They found a small office attached to one end of the kennels. A boy carrying a bucket of water was attending to the dog in the nearest run. He looked at them curiously. The dogs set up a loud barking as Priscilla and Hazel came closer.

Hazel knocked on the door of the office and then

pushed it open. It was a small room with photographs of dogs and with blue and red ribbons covering the walls. There was a big untidy desk and a file cabinet.

Hazel went back outside to ask the boy if she could see Mr. Detheridge.

"He's up to the house," the boy said. "Be back in a minute."

Priscilla watched him with the dogs. She didn't like the way he handled them, almost as if he disliked them. She wondered if it was because of him that Hassan had run away. She walked slowly along the length of the runs, looking carefully at the dogs.

She could see no sign of Hassan. Other dogs came up to the wire fencing to peer at her or to bark at her, and one elegant creature surveyed her coldly from her place on the top of the watering trough. There were runs on the other side of the kennel building too. Priscilla glanced back and saw Hazel talking to the boy. Mr. Detheridge had not appeared. She walked around the fencing to the other side.

Suddenly there was a wild barking, and there was Hassan, in the third run from the end, leaping at the fence trying to get to Priscilla. She ran to him and thrust her hands through the wire. He kissed her hands and threw himself at the fence. Priscilla was crying.

"Hassan, Hassan! You're all right, you're not run over, you're safe!" She put her face to the wire and felt his wet tongue slurping on her cheek. From his excitement she could tell he had heard them come, but in all the racket of barking she had not singled out his voice. She knelt beside the wire, talking and talking to him.

"Priscilla . . ."

She looked up and saw Hazel and a strange man. It went through her mind that this couldn't be Sonny Detheridge. He looked too old to be called Sonny, and he didn't look like the villain she had imagined. He was in fact a rather ordinary-looking middle-aged man in a pair of jodhpurs and a wrinkled white shirt under a heavy green cardigan.

But Hazel said, "This is my daughter, Mr. Detheridge."

The man frowned, looking faintly distressed. He said, "We'll have to go into the office. Can't hear yourself think out here." He struck at the wire fencing with the flat of his hand. "Get down, boy. Stop that noise."

Hassan yelped as the man's hand caught him on the end of his nose. He leaped back and then threw himself at the fence again.

The man took Hazel by the arm. "Come along." He moved her firmly away toward the office. "Come on, young lady," he said to Priscilla.

Priscilla leaned toward the frantic Hassan. "Don't, don't. We'll find some way. Be good, Hassan." She almost ran after her mother, wiping the tears away.

In the office the man said, "Well, there's not much I can say, Mrs. er . . ."

"Parkins," Hazel said.

"Yes. I was away when the dog got loose. Believe me, I've raised hell with the boy that let it happen. You probably saw him out there. I told him, when I got back, I said you find that dog or you're through in this business. That was one of my best stud dogs." He moved nervously around the small office, bumping his shin against his desk. He seemed like a harassed man.

"He was in terrible shape when we found him," Priscilla said. "He was starved and dirty and everything."

"I know, I can imagine. Terrible thing, a good dog like that. I told that boy, you find that dog . . . Well, then I heard somebody out near the Puddleford place had an Afghan. Just thought I'd take a look. I came across him last night, running across the field near the old bridge. Had the devil's own time catching him, I must say. Nearly broke my neck. But I was glad to see him. He's one of my best studs. Looks fine. You took good care of him." He kept nodding his head nervously.

"My daughter has cared for him since Labor Day," Hazel said.

"I'll be glad to reimburse her for her trouble—"

"Reimburse me!" Priscilla had had enough. "I love that dog. He loves me. How do you reimburse me for that? You didn't even let me know you'd taken him back."

"My dear child . . ." He spread his hands out. "I didn't even know you existed. I didn't know who you were or where you lived. As for the way you feel, I know that's a problem . . . I mean people get attached to dogs. Can't afford to do it myself. Strictly a business proposition with me, you understand." He sat down in the old wooden chair that pivoted. He smoothed his hair back. "Entirely business. I spend half the year, sometimes more, going all over the country to show my dogs. That's why I didn't know about the loss of the dog."

Hazel said, "Is the dog for sale, Mr. Detheridge?"

He looked startled. "For sale? Oh no, I shouldn't think so. I use him for stud, you see. I'd have to ask a big price if I sold him, to make it worth my while. He's a relatively young dog, three years old. He's got a lot of use left."

"Use." Priscilla turned away. "Let's go, Mother." The sooner she got out of here, the better. She felt as if she might hit Mr. Detheridge if she had to listen to him much longer. Use!

"Is there any price you would consider selling him for?" Hazel said.

Priscilla went out. There was no point in Hazel talking like that. Even if Hassan didn't cost much, they couldn't afford him. She got into the cab of the pickup and put her hands over her ears trying to shut out the sound of the dogs' barking, of Hassan's barking. She couldn't remember any day in all her life when she had felt so bad.

When they got home, Kath, Anne and Jimmy were there with Peter, waiting to hear the news. They listened with sad faces.

"Even Con Kelleher is out looking for Hassan," Anne said, "and we alerted a whole bunch of the people who ride every day."

Priscilla shook her head. "It's no use. He's found . . . and he's lost. For good."

Kath turned her head away to hide her tears.

"Mrs. Parkins," Anne said, "how much does Sonny want for him?"

"Six hundred dollars."

Priscilla gasped.

"He's out of his skull," Anne said. "I mean Hassan's a good dog, but he's not a big champion or anything."

"How do you know?" Jimmy said. "His kennel name wouldn't be Hassan."

"Mother says she's seen him at the shows. She can't remember exactly, but she thinks he came in second or third in his group at Madison Square last year. I mean he's an okay dog, but he's not a six-hundred-dollar dog."

"Mr. Detheridge says he uses him for servicing."

"Even so, that's a lot too much money. He's trying to take you."

"Well, that's Sonny Detheridge," Kath said.

"It doesn't make any difference whether he's worth six hundred or not," Priscilla said. "I don't have the money to buy him at any price." She nodded to her friends, biting her lip to keep it from trembling. "Thanks an awful lot for your help." She ran into the house. She picked up Hassan's dish and threw it into the trash can, and then she went into her room and closed the curtain. She lay stretched out on her bed trying not to think of the pressure of Hassan's warm back on the curve of her knees.

TWENTY-SIX

PRISCILLA spent most of Saturday and Sunday taking long walks and going skating by herself. Jimmy came over to skate with her late on Sunday, and Kath dropped in Sunday night for a few minutes and went away again, looking sad. Nobody referred to Hassan. It was as if there had been a death in the family.

The next week the house was in considerable confusion. The building inspector came out several times before he gave his approval to the work Paul had done. Then he came back one evening to go over Paul's plans for putting in electricity. This had to be done at once because the inspector considered the oil lamps a fire hazard. After the approval of plans, Paul was busy the remaining evenings and on the weekend to get the work done.

Hazel watched on Sunday, shaking her head. "They have made life so complicated," she said. "You can't lead a simple existence even if you want to."

"Well," Peter, who was helping Paul, said, "I guess an oil lamp could start a fire."

"Could and has," Hazel said, "but so have electrical shorts."

"Remember Mrs. O'Leary," Paul said, between the nails he held in his teeth.

"Who's she?" Peter said.

"Her cow kicked over a lantern and burned down Chicago."

"Oh. I thought she had something to do with a chowder."

Paul took the nails out of his mouth. "That was her sister, Mrs. Murphy."

"I just wonder," Hazel said. "I really do. Priscilla dear, get me the cookie sheet, just behind you, will you? These boys are going to be hungry."

Automatically, Priscilla got what her mother wanted and watched her mix up the cookie batter. Only half hearing them, she sat down to watch her father and Peter. She couldn't get her mind off Hassan. It wasn't just that she missed him so much; it was worry about him that kept her upset. He couldn't be happy in that disagreeable kennel with that careless boy and a man who didn't love his dogs. She knew he must be mourning for her.

"What I wonder is," Hazel said, "did oil lamps ever kill as many people as cars do?"

Paul and Peter laughed. "I know there's some thread of logic in your head somewhere," Paul said. "There always is."

Hazel beat the batter vigorously with a big wooden spoon. "We must not have oil lamps because we are now such a complex society, and we must think of the safety of others. All right. But—"

Peter finished it for her. "But did oil lamps ever kill as many people as cars do? Perfectly logical, Ma."

Hazel smiled. "You see." Later when she had taken the golden brown cookies from the oven she said, "I'm having lunch with Mrs. Alderson tomorrow.'

Priscilla stared at her. "Mrs. Alderson? Jackie's mother?"

"Somebody's mother. I'm not sure whose."

"Whatever for?"

Hazel smiled mysteriously. "The lodestone said 'Have lunch with Mrs. Alderson.' "

"I didn't even know you knew her."

"I met her the day I spoke at your school."

"Oh." Priscilla was not happy about the idea. Mrs. Alderson was the wife of the district judge, and she was president of the PTA. She was not the kind of person Hazel liked, or who usually liked Hazel. "I don't get it."

"You don't have to get it, Priscilla," Paul said rather sharply. "Your mother is simply having lunch with someone."

Priscilla felt unjustly rebuked. What had she said that was so awful? Nobody cared or even noticed that she was heartbroken. "Okay," she said, "I just asked. And I hope Hazel doesn't tell her she's lunching with her because the lodestone said to." She got up and grabbed her parka from the hook and went out. Nobody understood what she was going through.

She saw Kath starting across the meadow. Kath waved, but Priscilla pretended not to see her. She ran down to the river and started upstream, stamping through the snow-crusted bushes and sending up showers of snow. A partridge started up almost at her feet and flew across the river to the denser brush on the other side. When she came to the old stone bridge, she sat down on a flat stone that jutted out of the arch near the bottom. She swung her feet to keep them warm. The sky overhead was lead gray. Paul said it would snow before morning. There'd be snow for Christmas. A Christmas without snow would have seemed strange. Last year they had had over four feet by Christmas Eve. For a few minutes she felt home-sick for Lahti. But that was crazy. When she'd been there, her one dream had been to be in America. All right, she was here. But the house in Maine was gone, Hassan was gone. Wasn't anything ever the way you thought it would be?

She looked up quickly at the sound of feet crunching on snow. Paul was coming onto the bridge. He let himself down beside her, and she moved over to give him a little room on the stone.

"I needed a breath of air," he said.

She nodded.

"And I wanted to talk to you." He didn't go on for a minute.

Priscilla watched him nervously. Was he going to bawl her out for being rude to her mother?

"We are all very sorry, Priscilla, about the dog. We know what pain it gives you."

She thought, no, you don't.

"But I've said before, and I'll say again, you must realize when you have a pet that it's a chancy business. Animals don't live long; they die of old age at twelve or thirteen, or they get run over, or they run away, or whatever. When you love a pet, you have to accept these risks. You can't help feeling sad when something happens, but you can't allow it to throw your whole life out of kilter. What I'm saying, for that matter, applies to people as well. Grief comes to all of us, and it hurts. But we have to learn to control it, to live with it. We owe that to ourselves, and we owe it to the other people who love us or come into contact with us. We have to develop the strength to go on with the business of living even when it hurts the most. For instance, I loved my father very much." He glanced sideways at her and smiled. "You never really thought of him as my father, did you. He was your grandfather."

"But when you heard he'd died," she burst out, "you didn't even take a day off from work."

"No, I didn't. Work is therapy for me. You thought I didn't care that he'd died. Well, I . . ." He turned his head away for a moment. "I did."

"I'm sorry, Paul." She really was sorry. "I'm so wrapped up in myself, I never realized . . ."

He put his hand over her mittened one. "It's natural at your age. But you're growing up fast. It's a race to keep up, you know. A hard race. And Prissy, one other thing and then I'll stop lecturing. I've heard you make scornful remarks about Titania's lodestone several times. Don't you understand what the lodestone really is?"

"It's a superstition."

"Perhaps, in a way. But it's much more. It's the

tangible thing Titania clings to when she needs her greatest strength and wisdom—and that means usually when she needs them for us. It helps her to think, to meditate, to see."

"When we were little, it was like the good fairy or something. But it's kind of embarrassing to have it talked about now."

He shook his head. "You don't see. Look, when anything worrying loomed up—like the time I lost my job in England because we couldn't get permission from the Home Office to stay any longer, or the time that drunk in Helsinki robbed me of the rent money—did you worry about those things? Did they scare you?"

"No."

"Why not?"

"Because Titania always said the lodestone would help us."

"And did things work out?"

"Yes, I guess they did."

"Titania has used the lodestone to protect us. It's a symbol, really, of her own strength, ingenuity and love, which she uses for all of us. You and Peter have grown up feeling fairly secure, I think, and it's mainly because of the lodestone. Do you see?"

"It's because you and Hazel love us and take care of us."

"But that's what the lodestone means. All your life it's said, 'We love you and protect you. Don't be afraid.' "

Priscilla thought about it for quite a while. She had never seen it that way before, but she realized now that Peter did. He might not have put it that way, but he felt it. I've been too literal again, she thought. "Yes, I guess I see what you mean."

"When you see Titania with the lodestone in her hands, it often means that she's trying to find in her mind the best way to look after us."

"After Peter and me, you mean. But shouldn't we start looking after ourselves?"

"Of course. But it won't hurt—it will never hurt—to know that Titania and the lodestone are behind you."

"Like having God on your side."

He smiled. "Much as I love Titania, I don't know that she's ready for deification. Let's say, like being on the side of the angels. Maybe we could get away with that." He stood up and beat his hands together. "It's cold out here. And I've got to get back to the positives and negatives." He held out his hand. "Let there be light." He laughed and turned away, striding up the bank with his long legs. He was gone before Priscilla could thank him for talking to her.

Although it grew very cold, as the day slipped toward an early evening, Priscilla sat on for some time longer, thinking about what Paul had said. She saw her mother in a new way, not really the way Paul saw her, but differently from the old childish taking-for-granted. She thought about Jimmy's enthusiasm for Hazel, and the Wentworths' obvious liking, and Mr. Puddleford's accolade, "That mother of yours is all right." She thought of the audience at Hazel's speech, and the women who wanted her to start a class. It all added up to a complete person whom she had never really looked at before.

T W E N T Y - S E V E N

C HRISTMAS at the castle! Paul and Hazel had decided to hold an open house three nights before Christmas. The lights were in and working, the Christmas tree (a living one that Paul and Peter had dug) was up and lighted, and the whole house seemed to Priscilla to radiate warmth and joy. Perhaps, she thought, because it seemed like their own house.

Invitations went out to the Wentworths, to the Puddlefords, to Jimmy and his parents, to the other two men who worked at the garage, and to Peter's boss at the drugstore. For several days all four of the Parkinses worked hard. The house smelled of evergreen and of baking cakes and cookies. Hazel bought out the Greek's supply of marinated herring and anchovies and stuffed olives. Paul rounded up the ingredients for a *glögg*. Peter went to Boston on the train and came home with fresh shrimp from the market, Scandinavian crisp bread, cans of smoked salmon, and *lut-fisk*.

The night before the party Hazel baked bread and

made *kalakukko*, a fish-and-pork mixture baked in a round-shaped rye bread. Priscilla made her own specialty, *karjalan piirakka*, a pastry filled with rice. Paul sliced cheese, made the complicated *glögg*, brought in logs that he had split for the fireplace. If only Hassan were here, Priscilla thought, it would be perfect. But she had tried to do as Paul said she must do, live with the fact that he was gone.

When the time came for the guests to arrive, Hazel came into the big living room with a taper to light the many candles she had put around the room. She looked very pretty, Priscilla thought, in a new dark green velvet skirt she had made for herself and a square-necked short-sleeved sweater of paler green with a thin gold thread running through it. Her hair was piled up on her head.

Priscilla went up to her and kissed her. "You look lovely."

The smile her mother gave her made her feel good. Together they made a last-minute check of the food on the long table and plumped up the cushions on the chairs. Hazel had brought home a long flat cushion that had once covered a sofa. She had found some material to cover it, and now it was placed on the floor in front of the fireplace. Peter plopped down on it and thrust a lighted spill under the logs in the fireplace. After a few sputters, the pine boughs caught, and in a minute the bigger logs began to burn.

"Before they all get here," Hazel said, "I want to tell you something. It's not important, but some of them may have heard, and I don't want it to come as a shock—especially to Prissy."

Alarmed, Priscilla said, "What is it?"

"I'm going to teach a class in transcendental meditation, after the new year."

Priscilla's eyes widened. "You're what?"

"Hey, that's great!" Peter said. "How'd they talk you into it?"

"Well, they just did." Hazel seemed a little nervous. "So far eleven people have signed up, so I'll probably eventually have to break them up into two groups. That means two evenings a week. I hope none of you mind." She was looking at Priscilla. "I told them I'm not really qualified, but they seem to want to know whatever I know." She shrugged. "I'll just have to do my best. Later, perhaps I can take that course at Harvard, so I can do a better job."

Paul said, "We're proud of you."

Hazel gave a little laugh. "Prissy isn't. It makes her very nervous, doesn't it, dear?"

"No, I mean, I'm just so surprised. You said you'd never do it."

"Circumstances alter cases."

"Hey, here come the merrymakers," Peter said. He ran to the door and peered out. "It looks like the Donaldsons. And I can see the Puddlefords starting across the meadow."

"Dr. Donaldson can't stay long," Hazel said. "He has a baby case. So I told them to come early."

And Mrs. Puddleford would insist on waiting till the first car had arrived, Priscilla thought. She put the idea of her mother's class in the back of her mind to think about later. She wasn't sure what her reaction to it was.

Jimmy was not with his parents. "He'll be along a little later," Mrs. Donaldson said. She gave Hazel and Paul a meaningful look, and it occurred to Priscilla that the delay might have to do with a Christmas present. Jimmy had been trying, not too subtly, to find out what she wanted. It would be fun to see what he had chosen. She'd bought him an album of 1938 jazz that she knew he wanted. That thought reminded her that she was supposed to start the stereo. She put on the records Paul had chosen, mostly Mozart and some classical guitar by John Williams, and then she went to the door to welcome Kath and her parents.

Neither Jimmy's mother nor Mrs. Puddleford had been in the house before. Hazel gave them what Peter called the grand tour, and Priscilla could hear Mrs. Donaldson saying over and over, "How unusual!"

Other guests came, ate, drank, talked, and still neither Jimmy nor the Wentworths had come.

"Jimmy is coming, isn't he?" Priscilla asked his father.

"Oh, sure. He wouldn't miss it." The doctor smiled at her. He was, she thought, a very nice man. "He just had a little business to attend to. You know Jimmy, always something."

Then the Wentworths came, and to Priscilla's overwhelming joy Hollister was with them. "Can't stay long," he said, shaking hands with her and looking at her with those beautiful, soul-shattering eyes. "I'd already promised to go to a thing at the club. But it's awfully nice to be here." Then he moved on to her mother, and she could only smile dazedly at Mrs. Wentworth and Anne. Mr. Wentworth, they explained, was in bed with a quinsy sore throat. Paul promised to send home some *glögg*, guaranteed to cure anything.

Priscilla thought it was a lovely party. She was quite content to sit and listen to the talk, to jump up and get more *glögg* or more food for the guests. Dr. Donaldson left, and she heard him tell Paul he hadn't enjoyed a party so much in a long time. "I hate these social wingdings," he said, "where the people that are there talk about the people that aren't, and everybody wants to consult me over a drink in the corner. This was a really nice party. Not a soul mentioned a single symptom."

After he had gone, Priscilla saw Peter look at his watch and then look at Hazel. She nodded, and Peter started for the door. Priscilla intercepted him. "Where are you going?"

Peter looked over her head. "Ah . . . um . . . I'm going to meet Jimmy."

"How do you know where he is?"

"Well, I have this preconceived idea that he might possibly be . . . uh . . . be right back, Sis." He darted past her and out the door.

People were looking at Priscilla and smiling. Something was up. Something to do with Jimmy. She looked at her mother and raised her eyebrows in a question.

Paul struck the side of a knife against his glass to get everyone's attention, although already most of them were giving it. "My wife has a small statement to make," he said.

"It's very brief," Hazel said. She was smiling. "Our

Christmas present for Priscilla happens to require delivering tonight."

"My present?" Priscilla was entirely bewildered. She was quite sure her parents were giving her a new coat. "Why tonight?"

"Well, the timing happens to be . . ." Kath said. She had caught hold of Hazel's hand, and she was laughing. She looked happy and excited.

"Yes, the timing happens to be . . ." Hazel looked past Priscilla to the front door. "The time is NOW!"

Before the last word died away, the front door burst open, Jimmy and Peter stood there laughing, and Hassan leaped into the room and straight into Priscilla's arms. She almost fell over backward with the force of the jump. Paul put out his arm quickly to brace her. Everybody was laughing and talking. Mr. Puddleford was hugging his wife, and one of the mechanics' wives was crying happily.

Jimmy stood beside Priscilla grinning broadly. "What a scene!" he said. "What schmaltz!"

Priscilla was hugging Hassan and crying and laughing. "Is he mine? Is he really?"

"Your mother's got the bill of sale to prove it," Jimmy said. He put his arm around both Priscilla and Hassan and hugged them.

Hollister was shaking hands with Paul and Hazel. "What a moment to exit on," he said. "I'm late already, but I had to see this." He leaned past Jimmy and kissed Priscilla on the cheek. "Merry Christmas, Priscilla."

She was too stunned and too happy to realize that Hollister had kissed her until some time later. After all the guests had gone except Jimmy and Kath, and when they and the Parkinses were sitting around the fire eating the last of what Mrs. Wentworth had called "the best food served at a party in this township since the Prince of Wales was here," Priscilla put her hand to her cheek and said, "Hey! Hollister Wentworth kissed me."

"If it takes you that long to react," Jimmy said, "my worries are over."

"Somebody had better tell me how I happen to have my dog back." She leaned against the rock base of one of Hazel's chairs.

"You tell, Jimmy," Hazel said.

"Well," Jimmy said, "your mother had this little fund that she could spend, you see. And we talked about how to get Hassan for a reasonable price. It was Anne who came up with the idea of sending me over to see what Detheridge would sell him to me for. I could play it cool, you see, whereas you guys wanted Hassan very badly and he knew it. I said what about his story on the stud fees, but Anne said Detheridge will always settle for cash in hand. So I amble in, looking like the impecunious youth that I am, and I say I'd like to buy an Afghan, about three years old, for a pet, not a show dog, because I knew Sonny wouldn't want the dog in competition. He shows me several and I play it lukewarm, full of criticisms, thoroughly obnoxious in my own inimitable way, and finally I say, 'What about that one?' Well, old Hassan almost gave the show away, because he recognized me and he started carrying on. So I say, 'Oh, my, hysterical type, isn't he? No, I wouldn't want a nervous tic like that.' "

Priscilla laughed and kissed the top of Hassan's head. He looked up at her with his intelligent, dark eyes. "You nut, Hassan."

"So he says, well, he says, dog isn't all that bad, pretty good dog as a matter of fact, won this and that at Westminster and Boston and so on. I say, well, I was planning to spend two hundred bucks, and I want a good dog for my money, not some hysterical neurotic that I've got to feed tranquilizers to. So he gets carried away then with trying to sell me this dog. And"— Jimmy lifted his hands—"he succeeded. I brought him home and transferred him to your mother . . . or you, actually. You'll be getting the papers in due course. It takes awhile."

Priscilla didn't want to say in front of Kath and Jimmy, "Where did Hazel get two hundred dollars?" But almost before she'd finished wondering, she knew. The class in transcendental meditation. She looked at her mother across the room, and they both smiled.

"I was on tenterhooks the whole time," Kath was saying. "I never thought they'd bring it off. It seemed like they'd need a miracle."

"Sometimes you can bring off miracles," Priscilla said, still looking at her mother, "if you're lucky enough to have Titania's lodestone."

715867

d
H 1802
ti

Call no.
j
H1802
ti

Accession no.
715867

WITHDRAWN